WAITING

A Story of Hope

Gavin Whyte

© Gavin Whyte, 2012
Gavin Whyte has asserted his right under the
Copyright Designs and Patents Act 1988 to be
identified as the author of this work.

Written for the three families: Cox, Bryce, and Powell.

The following story is what happens when fact and fiction meet. It's important to realise, though, that fact can sometimes be the more magical one of the two.

1

Normally in December, Christmas was the only thing we had to wait for. But that year was different. Dan had been ill for a few months and his test results were due.

It all started with a twitch in his left eye that wouldn't go away. He began to have double vision and sometimes his face went numb. The doctors gave him a walking stick because he couldn't balance properly. We made a joke out of it at first, even Dan laughed. He went to the hospital for tests nearly every week. The doctors didn't have a clue what was wrong with him. But then on December the nineteenth, they gave him the news.

That night it gave me a proper excuse to get out of the house. I left mum and dad yelling at each other, like always. My little sister, Jade, was happily playing with a group of cuddly toys on the sofa. I said goodbye to her and said I wouldn't be long. I shouted upstairs that I was going to see Dan, but they didn't hear me. I stepped outside into the rain and felt the cold drops bouncing off the top of my head. It had been wet and grey for a few days. I put my hood up and ran. Dan only lived ten houses away so I was there in about fifteen seconds, but that didn't stop me from getting soaked. I rang the doorbell and waited. I could hear his mum and dad talking in the kitchen. His dad answered. He was a giant of a man. His hands were massive and his smile showed all of his teeth.

'Hello there, Jamie,' he said. 'Come on in.'

He shook my hand and patted me on the shoulder, like he always did.

Dan's mum's eyes were swollen and heavy.

'He's upstairs, love,' she said.

I made my way upstairs and was surprised to hear him laughing. I tapped lightly on his door and walked in. He was sitting on his black swivel chair in front of his TV, watching *Fresh Prince of Bel-Air* on DVD. He spun around and I could tell by his eyes he had been crying, too.

'Well?' I said, sitting down on the end of his bed. 'What did they say?

He paused the DVD.

'It's not good,' he said.

I waited.

He looked at the TV and laughed, then shook his head as if he didn't believe what he was about to say.

'I have a brain tumour.'

I stared straight through him. We were both silent for what felt like ages. He turned and unpaused the DVD.

'Wait,' I said, causing him to pause the DVD again. 'What does that mean? Can they get rid of it? What did they say?'

'It's a grade three tumour, whatever that means. Doctor said it's aggressive. It's too big and too risky for me to have an operation, so...'

'So what happens now?'

'I start radiotherapy two weeks after Christmas. I have to have it five days a week for six weeks.'

'Will that do it? Will it get rid of it?'

He shook his head. 'Doctor said it'll only shrink it.'

I could feel my eyes starting to fill up and a lump forming in my throat.

'How can you be so... normal?' I said, wiping my eyes.

He shrugged his shoulders.

'I cried at the hospital. Mum and dad did, too. It was a big shock. It still is, but dad says we have to accept it. We have to face it and fight it, so that's what I'm going to do.'

'Aren't you scared?' I said, feeling a tear reach the corner of my mouth.

'I was, but I'm not now. If this is the way God wants to take me, then...'

I wiped my eyes and runny nose on the sleeve of my jumper.

Silence again.

'I don't know what to say,' I said. 'Is there anything I can do?'

'Just be normal. I don't want you feeling sorry for me.'

I nodded.

'Oh, and I'll let you tell Teddy. You know what he's like.'

I chuckled and sniffed.

'Remember when he cried at *Pete's Dragon*?' said Dan.

We both laughed.

'And *The Lion King*,' I said.

Dan held his stomach as he laughed. He always did that.

'You want to watch some *Fresh Prince*?' he said.

'OK.'

We watched a couple of episodes and laughed and acted as if nothing had changed.

2

It was nearly nine o'clock when I left. I told Dan I would see him the next day. We did our handshake that we had invented when we were eight. I told him he was going to be fine, but I couldn't help but think the worst. I went downstairs to say goodbye to his mum and dad. The TV was on in the living room but nobody was watching it. Their Christmas tree sat in the corner of the room. The lights on it were off. There were dozens of Christmas cards on the window sill. His mum and dad were sitting in silence at the dining room table, cups of tea in their hands. His dad got up and shook my hand. He patted me on the shoulder and thanked me for coming. His mum got up, tissue in hand. She was a short, chirpy lady, who always seemed happy. She wrapped her small, thin arms around me. I could smell her faint perfume.

'Thank you for coming, love,' she said. 'We'll get through this. God won't take him away from us so soon.'

'He'll be fine,' I said.

'He's lucky to have a friend like you,' she said. 'We could hear you both laughing up there. It was nice.'

'We were laughing at Fresh Prince of Bel-Air.'

'You lot and that show,' she said, rolling her eyes.

She unlocked the back door and gave me another hug. I said n-night and went outside into the cold rain. I zipped up my coat and put my hood up. The street lamps gave everything a dark orange glow. I looked up and felt the rain falling on my face. Nearly every house I walked past had their lights on and curtains open. I could see Teddy kneeling in front of the TV, watching something about dinosaurs. The lights on his Christmas tree were alternating from red to green, to blue, to yellow. I could see Mr Heator watching football. Mrs Heator was reading a book with Bash, their little Terrier, asleep on her knee. They only had a small tree beside the TV and wasn't lit up or anything. Then there was my new neighbour, Mr Legna, sitting in a chair next to a dimly lit table lamp. He looked peaceful, as if he had fallen asleep after reading. He introduced himself to me over the garden fence the day before.

I stopped outside my house. Dad was sitting on the couch, watching football with a beer in his hand. I could see mum's silhouette through the curtains in Jade's room. She must be trying to get her to sleep, I thought. All the usual Christmas decorations were up: the big tree in the corner of the living room; the fake candles in the window that flashed every couple of seconds; the fat Santa on the mantel piece that wished you a Merry Christmas every time you pressed the red button next to his black boot; all that and it still didn't feel like Christmas. I clenched my fists and wished that mum and dad would get along. I wished that they would stop arguing. I wished for them to get back to normal. I wished they were like Dan's parents.

3

Empty Carling cans were scattered on the kitchen worktop. Dirty dishes, cups and glasses were piled up in the sink. I rinsed out a glass and poured myself some milk. I went into the living room and sat in the chair, closest to the TV. Dad didn't look at me; he was glued to the football.

When the ref gave a corner, I told him that Dan had got his test results.

He looked at me and took a swig of his beer. I had a sip of my milk.

'What's up with him then?'

The whistle blew for a penalty and he jumped out of his seat, cheering, spilling beer on the carpet. It soaked in, a bubble at a time.

'Brain tumour,' I said, finally.

He dipped his head. He bit his bottom lip and scratched his nose. He noticed the brown beer stain on the carpet and pushed his big toe into it.

'I'm sorry to hear that. Danny's a good lad. He doesn't deserve that.'

I pretended to watch the football.

'Are you OK?' he said.

'Yeah, I guess.'

I finished my milk, climbed the stairs and found mum sitting on her bed, looking at some old photos. Some were laid out on the duvet. There was one of me when I was a couple of weeks old and one of Jade, too, when she was born. There were a couple of mum and dad on their wedding day, and one of nan and grandad, sitting on a bench at Bridlington, holding ice creams.

'Hello, love,' said mum. 'I'm just going through some oldies. Look at this one.'

It was a photo of me and grandad at the park. He had his arm around me and was laughing. I was grinning without my two front teeth. He was wearing his favourite brown trousers. They were stained with smudges and specks of white paint and had fag holes burnt into them.

'Good memories, eh?' she said.

I smiled and nodded.

'Look at his trousers,' she said. 'Scruffy beggar. No matter how many times I asked him, he just wouldn't throw them away.'

She laughed quietly to herself.

'Oh, I forgot, how's Dan?'

I put the photo next to me on the bed.

'Not good,' I said.

My eyes filled up.

'Here, come and sit,' she said, patting the bed. 'What's wrong with him?'

She handed me a tissue from her pocket, but I just held it. I took a deep breath and told her the news. She started crying. She said she was sorry and how cruel life could be. She said she couldn't even begin to imagine how his parents felt.

'How's he coping?' she said.

I shrugged my shoulders. 'He said he cried in the hospital, but said if that's the way God wants to take him, then...'

'Oh, I'm so sorry.'

'He starts radiothrapy two weeks after Christmas.'

'You mean, radiotherapy, love. Poor Dan. I can't believe it. So young. So close to Christmas, too. I know he's been poorly for a while but I didn't expect this. I'll buy a Get Well Soon card for him. I know it won't help much, but at least it shows we're thinking of him. When you seeing him next?'

'Tomorrow.'

'OK, I'll get one in town tomorrow morning. I'll let you take it round. I haven't seen his mum and dad in ages; I'd feel a bit awkward if I took it.'

'OK, no worries.' I yawned.

'Get to bed. Get some rest.'

'Can I say goodnight to Jade?'

'Yes. Be quiet, though. I've only just got her to sleep. She was asking where you were. She's been playing with her imaginary friends all day. A vivid imagination, has that one.'

Mum hugged me and kissed my cheek.

'What a Christmas this is going to be, eh?' she said.

I picked up the photo of me and grandad. 'Can I take this?'

'Of course. Put it under your pillow; see if he comes to you in your dreams.'

I tiptoed into Jade's room. She was fast asleep. I listened to her breathing. The floor creaked when I moved and she opened her eyes. She looked up at me and stretched.

'They're with Dan,' she said.

I stared at her, confused.

'What? Who's with him?'

She smiled, slowly shut her eyes and went back to sleep.

4

I lay in bed looking at the photo of me and grandad. I closed my eyes and tried to remember him, but I couldn't. Thoughts of Dan had pushed everything out. I put the photo under my pillow, like mum had said, and wished grandad would come and visit me in my dreams. Shadows of monsters and witches danced wildly on my wall, all in time with the tree outside. I used to be scared of them, but not anymore. I knew they weren't real.

That night I dreamt I was running through the streets in the pouring rain. The rain wasn't touching me, though; I was dry. I looked in people's houses and saw everyone standing at their windows. I ran up to Mr Legna and he was looking up at the sky. I ran to Teddy and tried shouting his name, but my voice had disappeared. He was staring straight through me as if I wasn't there. I ran through a puddle but there were no ripples and my feet stayed dry, too. I got to Dan's house and he was standing there, staring at me, just like Teddy had been. He was crying, though. There was a tall, dark shadow behind him. I knew it was evil, I could feel it. It was getting closer and closer to him. I started to bang on the window, shouting at him to turn around, but nothing came out of my mouth. I felt a tugging on my coat. I looked down and saw Jade, shaking her head. I ignored her and carried on hitting the window, trying to get Dan to turn around. I tried and tried and tried. Then the shadow surrounded him.

'Jamie. Jamie, love.'

I opened my eyes and mum was shaking me. My heart was thumping and my pillow was cold with sweat.

'You were banging on the wall,' she said. 'Did you have a nasty dream?'

'Erm... yeah. Maybe.'

5

I woke up wishing that Dan's diagnosis had just been a nightmare. The photo was still under my damp pillow. I couldn't remember if grandad had come to me in my sleep or not. I sat up and looked outside. It had stopped raining and the sun was out. Mr Legna walked past. He saw me, smiled and waved. I waved back but didn't smile. I went downstairs and found mum in the kitchen, washing the pile of dishes and cups and glasses that had been in the sink. There was a carrier bag full of empty Carling cans, waiting to be taken out to the bin.

'Morning,' she said. 'Did you get back to sleep all right last night?'

'I think so.'

'You must've been shattered; look at the time. Get some breakfast. I'll put the kettle on and make you a cup of tea.'

'Thanks.'

I sat in the living room with Jade, watching cartoons and eating my cereal. She was sitting on the sofa, having some toast. Her feet dangled over the edge, nowhere near the floor.

'Are you better?' she asked.

'What do you mean?'

'You were shouting and banging. I heard you.'

'Oh, yeah. I'm OK now. Jade, can you remember what you said last night?'

She shook her head.

'You woke up and said somebody was with Dan. Don't you remember?'

'No,' she said, not taking her eyes off the TV. 'Will you bake with me today?'

'Maybe. I have to go and see Teddy.'

'Jamie's busy at the moment, love,' said mum, walking in, holding my cup of tea with a steady hand. 'I'll make some buns with you after we've been to town. OK?'

She nodded.

'Where's dad?' I said.

'He's working today, thank God,' said mum.

I looked at her.

'I'm sorry. I didn't mean that. It's just... we're going through a bit of a rough patch at the moment.'

I blew my tea.

'Every couple has their ups and downs,' she said. 'It's natural. We'll sort it out.'

'When?' I said.

'I don't know, but we will. Do you want to come to town with me and Jade today?'

'Maybe.'

'You don't have to if you don't want to.'
'Maybe. I'll see.'
'Well, if you don't want to, just say,'
'Mum, *may*be!'

She returned to the kitchen like a puppy who had been told off.

Jade looked at me with eyes that said go and apologise.

Mum was just about to take the rubbish outside.

'I'm sorry,' I said.
'It's OK, love, I understand.'
'I'll come to town with you.'
'Good,' she said, looking pleased. 'It might help take your mind off things for a while.'

6

Kingsgate shopping centre was jam packed. There was no space to move at all. Everybody was in such a rush. The queues looked like snakes of people. Shop assistants got yelled at for not having things in stock and were blamed for ruining Christmas. Screaming babies in prams got whizzed through the crowds. Parents told their kids off for touching things that they weren't supposed to touch. Mum told Jade to walk in between us and to hold our hands. That way we wouldn't lose her.

Outside was sunny but freezing. We had our gloves, hats and scarves on. Mum bought us a cup of hot chocolate from Dunker's Delight. We sat on a bench outside the Parish Church and drank it. I could feel it warming me up from the inside out. I looked at the names of the people who were buried beneath our feet. Pigeons gathered round us, hoping that we might have a crumb to spare. Jade told them that we didn't have anything and shoo'd them off. Mum laughed at her. I took a long slurp of my thick, milky hot chocolate.

'Nice, eh?' said mum.
'Very,' I said.

We set off to look for a card for Dan. There were so many to choose from. Mum held up the two she liked the most.

'The football one,' she said, 'or this one with the car?'

'Definitely the car, but isn't there a funny one?' I said.

'I don't want to get him a funny one, Jamie. Maybe if it was just from you, but not from the whole family.'

'Then can we get him two?'

'I suppose so. Which one do you want?'

I picked one with a chimp on it, sitting on a toilet. It was holding a Get Well Soon card in one hand, and in the other hand it held a bare toilet roll tube. It said *"Don't look in this card if you don't want to see what I've used it for."* Then when you opened it, it said in big letters, *"YOU REALLY ARE SICK! GET WELL SOON!"*

Mum looked at the card and then at me. 'You dirty beggar,' she said and smiled.

We went to a stationery shop and mum bought Jade a magazine. It came with free stickers. She bought me a Smooth Glide: a DIY glider. On the box it said it could fly up to 20 metres.

The bus was full on the way home. There was a kid drawing a huge face in the condensation covered window. There was a girl at the front playing naughts and crosses by herself. Every naught and every cross had drips running down from them. Her mum told her to stop it, saying the windows weren't for drawing on. There was a woman wiping away a perfect circle. When she finished she put her eye to it and spied at the world passing by. An old man pressed the bell and motioned for mum to take his seat. She said thanks and sat down. Jade climbed onto her knees. The man said that mum had a little angel with her. Jade ignored him, though, and continued to look at her magazine through the plastic wrapper. I held on to the bars and swayed back and forth. The bus finally came to a halt. The old man winked at me as he walked past. An old lady behind mum got off, too, so I sat down in her seat. It was warm and I could still smell her thick perfume. The bus stopped at the next stop. An old man struggled to get on. He reminded me of grandad, with his grey thin hair and frail body. He kept on blowing into his hands to warm up his fingers. They looked like uncooked sausages. He looked around for a seat. Mum whispered for me to get up for him. I stood up and pointed to my seat. He carefully made his way down the centre of the bus. The driver noticed him in his rear-view mirror and slowed down.

'Thanks, lad,' he said, sitting down. 'Needs to be more like you.'

Mum smiled and looked proud.

When we got home, we wrote the cards for Dan and his family.

Mum licked the seal of the envelope.

'There you go,' she said. 'It's nothing much, but at least it shows them they're in our thoughts.'

'I'll take both cards around later,' I said. 'I need to go to Teddy's first and tell him what's going on.'

'OK. Have some lunch first, though, eh? I'll make us all a sandwich.'

Jade was in the living room, looking through her magazine. She was peeling off stickers and putting them onto random pages.

'Which one do you want?' she said.

I shrugged. 'Surprise me.'

I sat down and she told me to shut my eyes. I felt her little thumb pressing down on my forehead. She giggled. I opened my eyes and looked in the mirror, above the fireplace. There was a pair of white wings stuck to my head.

'Thanks, Jade.'

Mum came in holding a tray of egg and cress sandwiches and cups of tea. She looked at me and started to laugh.

'What are you two dafties up to?' she said.

'Jamie has wings,' said Jade. 'Big white wings.'

7

Mum and Jade were just starting to bake when I left to go to Teddy's. Jade was standing on a buffet so she could reach the kitchen worktop. Mum was trying to get some baking trays from the back of the cupboard.

'Got your gloves?' she said, from inside the cupboard.

'Yeah,' I said.

'And your hat?'

'Yup.'

'What about the cards?'

'It's a Sunday, Dan'll be at church. I'll take them round tonight.'

I headed for the door.

'Excuse me,' said mum, pointing to her cheek.

Jade copied her.

I gave them both a kiss on the cheek.

'That's better,' said mum. 'See you soon. And good luck with Teddy.'

Teddy's house was half way between Dan's and mine. He lived with his grandparents, who he called his mum and dad. He never knew his real dad and had only spoken to his real mum a couple of times. It never seemed to bother him, though.

I walked past Mr Legna's house and looked in but he wasn't there.

I reached Teddy's semi-detached house. The silver birch in the centre of the garden always prevented the living room from getting any sunlight. His mum and dad had planted it from a seed when they moved in. I knocked on Teddy's door. No answer. I knocked harder. Teddy's head slowly appeared out of the open landing window.

'Oh, it's you,' he said, looking down at me. 'Wait a sec.'

I could hear him running down the stairs.

'I thought you were a salesman,' he said, opening the door. 'Mum and dad have just gone out. They said they'd seen a guy going to next-door's. I'm not supposed to answer it if he comes here.'

'I haven't seen anyone,' I said.

He invited me in and quickly shut the door.

'Do you want a drink?'

'Nah, I'm good, thanks.'

I followed him into the living room. The walls were covered with Teddy's school photos. There was a cabinet full of World War Two models: tanks, planes, ships, guns and little soldiers. They were all covered in a thin layer of fluffy, grey dust.

Teddy saw me looking at them. 'Dad loves his models,' he said 'Have you heard anything about Dan?'

'That's kind of why I'm here,' I said, sitting down on the springless sofa. 'It's not good news.' I took a deep breath. 'Dan's got cancer. A brain tumour.'

Teddy looked into space, not saying a word.

Finally, he said, 'He's going to be OK, though, right? I mean, they can get rid of it, can't they?'

I shook my head and told him what Dan had told me.

'Shit,' he said, scratching his head.

I could hear the house creak and moan as the central heating came on.

'What do we do now, then?' he said, looking uncomfortable.

'Dan wants us to act like normal.'

'Like normal?'

'What else can we do? We just have to be there for him, no matter what.'

'This sucks. It really sucks.'

'I'm going to take a card round later. You want to come?'

He sighed and picked his nail. 'OK. I guess I'd rather go with you than by myself.'

'Right. I'll come for you around seven thirty. He'll be back from church then.'

'That's fine,' he said. 'You sure you don't want a drink? Go on, have one.'

*

I didn't stay at Teddy's long. It was hard to talk to him. Suddenly everything had changed. I was heading out of the driveway when an overly enthusiastic salesman came up to me.

'Do you live here, my friend?' he said. He looked all happy and excited for no reason. 'Is there anyone in that I can speak to?'

I looked over my shoulder and saw Teddy quickly disappearing behind the curtains.

'No, I don't live here,' I said. 'There is someone in, though. Just keeping knocking until he comes.'

'Much appreciated, lad. Thanks a bunch.'

The happy salesman went and pounded nonstop on Teddy's door. Teddy appeared at the window, looking annoyed. I laughed and he gave me the finger and I laughed even more.

8

When I got home, mum and Jade were just clearing up after baking. The sweet, buttery smell of hot dough filled the kitchen. Jade was covered in icing sugar. It was all over her hands and face and in her hair.

'Smells good,' I said, throwing my trainers under the stairs. 'What have you made?'

'Butterfly buns,' said Jade. 'Look at this one! Look how big it is!'

'There's more icing sugar on her than on the buns,' said mum. 'How was Teddy?'

'Yeah, he's OK,' I said. 'I was surprised at how calm he was.'

'He'll be in shock. People deal with this kind of thing in different ways.'

'You want a bun?' said Jade. She stood on her tiptoes, reaching over and grabbing one. 'There you go.'

I took a bite of the soft, warm sponge.

'You'll be a good baker one day,' I said.

She beamed and rubbed her hands together.

I grabbed another bun and went to my room. I sat on my bed and worked on the glider that mum had bought me. I followed the instructions and put it together, piece by piece.

I put the stickers on in the correct places. I threw it across my room and hit my wall, dinting its nose.

'Where're you going now?' said mum. 'You've only just got in.'

'I'm going gliding,' I said, showing her the glider. 'My room isn't big enough.'

I went round the back, down the steps, onto the wet grass. The only thing in the way was the empty washing line. I threw the glider and watched it fly all by itself. It flew across the lawn, over the washing line, over the fence and into Mr Legna's garden. I ran to the edge of the lawn but couldn't see it anywhere. I stepped over dad's bare flowerbed and grabbed the fence, leaping over onto Mr Legna's long, drenched grass. It was covered with dead leaves, twigs, and brown rotten apples, that had fallen from his tree. Twigs snapped beneath my long, high strides. I looked in the naked branches of the apple tree and even behind the ancient shed. I couldn't see my glider anywhere.

'You won't find it looking there,' said a voice.

I was Mr Legna.

He was standing at the top of his garden steps, next to the coal shed. He wore a brown and red woolly jumper that was frayed at the cuffs. He was holding a blue mug with both hands and the steam from it was rising past his crinkled face. His eyes were a sparkling blue.

'It's Jamie, isn't it?' he said.

'Yeah. I'm sorry. I've lost my glider in your garden.'

'I know you have. I saw it flying in.'

'Where is it? Where did it land?'

'It's right under your nose,' he smiled.

I looked through the grass and there it was, covered in dirt and a few tiny snails. I picked it up and noticed the left wing had snapped off.

'Damn thing,' I muttered.

'Come inside,' he said. 'I'll fix it for you.'

His kitchen was like a cave. It took my eyes a while to get used to the dim light. The cupboards were dark green and the worktop was the colour of wet sand. The stove in the corner was giving off a lot of heat but hardly any light. I could see the flames licking the square glass panel. It was just like what my grandad used to have in his kitchen; pieces of wood were stacked along the side with the odd lump of coal.

'Take a seat,' he said, pointing to a little white wooden stool, in between the oven and the stove. He held a bag of small brown sweets in front of me. 'Cough sweet? They're good for this time of the year.'

'Thank you,' I said, taking one. It was sweet and spicy.

He opened a stubborn drawer and pulled out a small glue stick. He took the broken glider from my hands and began putting small dabs of glue on the severed wing. He stuck it into place and steadily handed it to me.

'Hold it tight,' he said. 'No sudden movements.'

He took a sip of his drink and his eyes scanned me.

'How come you're not with your friends today?' he said.

'I've just been to see Teddy and Dan's at church.'

'Church?' he said, sounding surprised. 'Not many young'uns go to church nowadays.'

'He's a Christian. His dad's a pastor at their church.'

He took another sip of his drink.

'Are you religious, Jamie?'

I shook my head.

'What about your parents?'

'My dad *def*initely isn't. He says that sort of thing's for wackos.'

He chuckled.

'Mum mentions God more since grandad died,' I said, 'but I wouldn't say she's religious.'

'Well you don't have to be religious to believe in God.'

My hands fell loose. Mr Legna gave a little whistle and pointed to the glider.

'The glue hasn't dried yet,' he said.

He finished his drink and poured a bit of cold water into his cup. He swirled it round, walked over to his back door and threw the dregs outside, onto the grass.

'Green tea leaves,' he said, catching me watching him. 'Just returning them to the earth, where they came from.'

I let go of the wing and it stayed attached.

'Thanks,' I said.

'Don't fly it again today, though,' he said. 'Let it heal.'

I stood up and walked towards the door.

'Thanks again.'

He nodded slowly. 'Any time.'

*

Mum was sitting on the sofa, reading the newspaper. Jade was next to her, fast asleep, covered in a green blanket. Mum whispered that I had been a while. I told her that the glider had landed in Mr Legna's garden and the wing had snapped off, but he fixed it for me.

'I didn't know we had a new neighbour,' she said.

'He only moved in the other day, I think.'

'When I get the time, I'll go and introduce myself. Maybe take him round some buns.'

Jade mumbled something in her sleep and mum pulled the blanket over her shoulders.

9

Dad had been home for fifteen minutes and he and mum still hadn't spoken. They walked past one another in the dining room as if neither one of them existed. Dad warmed up his dinner in the microwave and sat at the table. He read the newspaper whilst eating. I was sitting in the living room with Jade and mum, watching TV. Jade got up and went to see him.

'Hello, Princess,' I heard him say. 'Have you had a good day?'

I heard her tell him about town and the hot chocolate and the pigeons in the church yard. She told him about her magazine and the butterfly buns she'd made. He said he would have one after his dinner, and he would look at the magazine with her before she went to bed. She came back into the living room and sat next to mum. I wanted to go and speak to dad, just like Jade had done. I wanted to tell him about my glider and how Mr Legna had fixed it for me. I wanted to tell him about how I'd left Teddy with the salesman.

I heard him placing his knife and fork on his empty plate and sliding it to one side. He stood in the doorway, drinking a can of coke. To mum, he was invisible.

'How's Dan?' he said to me.

'I haven't seen him today. He's been at church all day.'

He didn't say anything and went upstairs and ran himself a bath.

10

Teddy answered his door as soon as I knocked. He shouted to his mum and dad that he was leaving and they told him to be careful and not to be too late. He was wearing his red and black woolly hat that his mum had made him when we were in Junior School.

'Nice hat,' I said.

'Piss off.'

I laughed.

We set off walking to Dan's house. It was icy cold and the sky was full of stars. We could see our breath when we exhaled. Teddy put his thumb and finger together and pretended he was smoking a fag.

'How're things with you?' he said.

'Been better.'

'Me too. How're your mum and dad? Still arguing?'

I nodded.

'What about yours?' I said.

'Well, they're arguing but mum's losing it a bit, too. She keeps on repeating things over and over again, and I swear her hearing's going. Dad says it's just what happens when you get to that age.'

I kicked a pebble. It bounced off a curb, just missing a car.

'Ooo, close,' he said. 'I'm sure she'll be fine, though. She always tells me stories about the war and how she met dad. It's always the same bloody stories, like, but still...'

We got to Dan's house and he invited us in.

'It's freezing,' he said. 'Oh, nice hat, Teddy.'

I laughed.

'Don't *you* start,' said Teddy.

We followed Dan into the living room. He was using his walking stick. Teddy gave me a worried glance.

'I take it Jamie told you, Teddy?' said Dan.

Teddy nodded and looked embarrassed.

'I need you to act like normal. OK?'

'It's weird, though,' said Teddy. 'It's like... it's like it's not real. Like it's not actually happening.'

'I wish it wasn't real,' said Dan.

'Things like this don't happen to people our age.'

Dan shrugged. 'Looks like they do.'

'How was church?' I said. 'Did you tell the people there?'

Dan nodded. 'It was awful, but nice, too. They're super kind people and they care a lot.'

'Did they cry?' said Teddy.

I elbowed him.

'What? I'm just asking.'

'Yes, Teddy,' said Dan. 'A few did. They're like family, you know.'

Teddy and I nodded.

'Anyway, do you want a drink?'

'Yeah, OK,' said Teddy.

'Me, too,' I said.

Dan picked up his walking stick and struggled to get up off the sofa.

'I'll get them,' I said, standing up.

'No,' he said. 'I'll get them. Remember what I said; just act like normal.'

I sat back down and he hobbled past us, towards the kitchen.

Teddy looked at me and whispered, 'He's got worse since the last time I saw him.'

'Shh,' I said, and flicked his cold, red ear.

He yelped out loud. '*Id*iot. My ears are *freez*ing!'

We could hear Dan laughing at us in the kitchen.

He came in holding one glass of orange.

'You know when I said just act like normal?' he said.

'Yeah,' I said.

'Well you can go and bring your own drinks. I can't be bothered making three trips.'

'That's fine,' I said, laughing.

I got our drinks and noticed the calendar on the wall. On the nineteenth it said, *fingers crossed* in red pen. It was Dan's writing.

Dan's mum came downstairs and stood in the doorway, looking at the three of us.

'Hello, boys,' she said. 'Why are you all drinking orange juice? It's freezing out there. You should've got some hot milk or hot chocolate, or at least a cup of tea.'

Teddy looked at me and whispered hot milk.

'Orange is fine, thanks,' I said. 'Ignore him.'

'You start your radiotherapy in three weeks, don't you, love?' she said, smiling at Dan.

He nodded.

'Would you like to go with him one day, boys?'

We both nodded.

'That's good of you. Only one at a time, though. When his dad's at work, the hospital'll send a taxi to take us there and back. The taxi picks up other patients, too, and takes them to the hospital, so we don't want to take up too many seats.'

'That's OK,' I said.

'I'll leave you boys to it,' she said, backing out of the room.

'Your mum's great,' said Teddy.

'My right arm's starting to go a bit weird,' said Dan. 'It's like I can't use it properly. My mum's been helping me put my eye drops in, the ones I got from the hospital. They're to help me with the double vision.'

He suddenly started to laugh hysterically. Teddy and I looked at one another, confused.

Dan calmed down himself and continued. 'This morning, though, she slipped and poked me in the eye with the bottle!'

He laughed until tears were streaming down his face. His hands were on his stomach.

'It's not even funny!' he said, laughing more.

Both Teddy and I started to giggle. Within seconds, all three of us were laughing our heads off.

'Stop it,' said Teddy. 'I'm dying here!'

We all stopped laughing. There was complete silence.

'I didn't mean that,' said Teddy, worried.

Dan looked at me, then at Teddy.

'I'm sorry,' said Teddy. 'I didn't-'

Dan burst into a fit of laughter that was even louder than before.

'Don't do that to me!' said Teddy, laughing nervously.

11

It was nine o'clock when we left Dan's house. Teddy didn't say much on the way home.

'You OK?' I said.

He didn't say anything.

Hoping to get a smile out of him, I asked him what the salesman wanted.

He stopped walking.

'What if he dies, Jamie?'

I took a deep breath and blew up to the starry sky. I watched my breath disappear like a ghost in the night.

'He'll be fine,' I said.

We started walking again.

'Seeing the difference in him tonight made me realise it's actually happening; then his mum's asking us if we want to go to the hospital with him, I don't know if I can do that.'

'I know how you feel, Teddy. I don't *want* to go to the hospital but I'll do it for Dan.'

Teddy seemed lost in thought.

'I had a nightmare last night,' I said.

'What about?'

'I was outside Dan's. He was just standing at the window, looking at me, crying. There was this shadow behind him, getting closer and closer. I can remember shouting his name and telling him to turn around, but there was no sound coming out of my mouth. It was weird.'

'Then what happened?'

'I woke up just as the shadow was about to surround him.'

'Shit. I hope I don't have any nightmares.'

'Ask your mum to tell you one of her stories.'

'Think I'd prefer a nightmare.'

We both laughed.

We did our handshake and then he suddenly wrapped his arms around me. I stood still with my arms by my side.

'Cheers, man,' he said, and turned around and walked swiftly down his driveway.

*

I walked the rest of the way home amazed at how bright the stars were. I tried counting them but soon forgot which ones I'd already counted.

'Beautiful night,' said a voice ahead of me.

It was Mr Legna. He was sitting on his garden wall, surrounded by the orange glow of the street lamp.

'Have you seen the stars?'

He nodded, smiled and looked up. 'It's good to see a young one like yourself appreciating one of the world's most splendid shows.'

I looked up again.

'Imagine,' he said, 'if the stars only came out once every fifty years, people would gather round and celebrate. They would treat the stars as if they were something out of this world. This amazing spectacle happens every night, yet the majority of people stay indoors, glued to the TV. They have no idea what they're missing. Nothing here lasts forever.'

He headed back towards his house.

'Good night, Jamie.'

12

Mum and dad were watching the news. Mum was sitting on the sofa with a glass of white wine in her hand, and dad was on the chair closest to the door. A couple of empty Carling cans were next to him on the floor, along with an empty packet of peanuts.

'You look cold,' said mum. 'Come and sit next to the fire.'

'I'm OK,' I said.

'How's Dan?'

'He's fine. We had a laugh tonight. It was all right.'

She smiled and had a sip of her wine.

'He's a brave one, is that,' she said.

I could tell they still weren't talking to each other.

'I think I'll get off to bed,' I said.

'You'll make a better door than a window,' said dad.

'What?'

'I can't see the TV. Why don't you sit down?'

'Nah, I'll go to bed.'

'OK, love,' said mum.

I threw my coat and hat on my bed. I looked at my glider and Mr Legna's handy work. It was as if it had never been broken.

Jade called my name.

I tiptoed to her room. She shielded her eyes from the landing light when I walked in.

'You OK? I whispered.

'Dan's on his way,' she said. 'They're with him. He'll be OK.'

I knelt down beside her bed.

'Jade, what do you mean?'

'They told me you don't have to worry. Everything's OK.'

'*Who* told you?'

'*They* did.'

She shut her eyes and turned on her side.

I backed out of her room and shut her door quietly. I sat on my bed and thought about what she had said. I thought of Dan and what it would be like if he died. I thought about his funeral. I slammed my face into my pillow and started to cry. I could feel the cotton getting all wet and cold. I felt a hand rest on my shoulder and my mattress sag.

'You OK?' said dad.

I wiped my eyes and nose and nodded.

'Get some sleep, OK?'

13

That night the yelling didn't stop until eleven o'clock. Mum was shouting at dad, saying he was stubborn and selfish. Dad said how much she had changed since grandad had died. He said he didn't know her anymore. There was the odd gap of silence until they started again. I tossed and turned and tried covering my ears with my pillows, but I could still hear them. I got out of bed and leaned on the window sill. Outside seemed so quiet and calm. I opened my window ajar and could smell how fresh the night air was. I took a deep breath, shut my eyes and exhaled for as long as I could. I looked up at the stars and thought about grandad.

'Where did you go?' I whispered.

I looked at the black space between the stars and, as if from nowhere, more stars slowly appeared.

'Can you hear me, Grandad?'

I got the photo and began telling him about everything. I spoke to him as if he was sat next to me. I spoke to him the way I used to, before he got ill. I told him about Dan and how scared I was that he might die. I told him about Jade and how she said things in her sleep. I told him about Mr Legna and how kind and strange he was. I told him about mum and dad and how fed up I was with them.

I heard either mum or dad on the landing. I got back into bed and pulled the duvet to my chin. My door handle squeaked and the thin line of light grew on my ceiling. I shut my eyes and pretended I was asleep. I heard my window being shut and then felt a kiss on my forehead.

I pretended to stir and stretch. I opened my eyes and saw no-one. I sat up and looked around. My door was slightly open but someone had shut the window, just as I had heard. I went and peered onto the dark landing. I stood at the top of the stairs and looked down.

'What are you doing, love?' said mum from behind me.

She was standing next to the window. The light from the moon made her look like a spirit.

'Have you just been into my room?' I said.

'No, why?'

I frowned. 'Somebody was... in my-'

'It's late, Jamie. You'll have been dreaming. Go on, get back to bed.'

I climbed into bed and mum shut my curtains. She picked up the photo off the window sill.

'Put this under your pillow,' she said. 'You never know, eh.'

14

It was the first Christmas without grandad. I wondered if it would be the last Christmas with Dan. I remembered how much fun it was last year and how things had changed so quickly.

It was seven o'clock when Jade came into my room. She had planned on leaving Santa some carrots and a glass of milk, but dad persuaded her to leave some salted peanuts and a can of Carling instead; she was desperate to see if Santa had taken them.

We crept downstairs and opened the living room door. Her face lit up. She covered her mouth to stop herself from screaming. She ran towards the presents, piled high on one side of the sofa. She didn't even see the clean bowl and empty can; proof of Santa's visit.

'Are these mine?' she said, looking at the labels.

'I think so.'

There was a stack of presents on the chair and two small piles on the floor, at either side of the fireplace.

'These are yours,' she said, picking one up from the chair. 'Look. Look. Here's your name.'

I sat down on the other side of the sofa and watched her go through all her presents. She started jumping up and down.

'Can I open one?'

'We have to wait until mum and dad get up,' I said. 'They won't be long.'

'Pleeeease. Just a peep at one? Just one. Pleeeease.'

'OK, just one. But only a peep.'

She picked up a small box. It was wrapped in red and white striped paper.

'Snow globe,' she whispered to herself.

She put her finger in one of the corners and ripped it.

'That's enough,' I said.

'What's going on here?' said mum, poking her head around the door.

Jade quickly hid the present behind her back.

We laughed at her.

'Cheeky beggar,' said mum. 'I see you've already opened the snow globe.'

*

Dad came down not long after and we all opened our presents together. They still weren't properly talking to one another, but dad asked mum if she wanted a bacon sandwich for breakfast which made her smile. Within minutes, the whole house smelt of sizzling bacon.

For most of the morning, I played with Jade with all of her new toys and games. Dad worked in the kitchen, getting the Christmas dinner ready, whilst mum tidied up the house. That's what happened every year.

'Don't you think it's time you two got dressed?' said mum, picking up the torn wrapping paper from the floor and putting it in a black bin bag.

'No,' said Jade.

Mum looked at her, eyebrows raised.

'OK,' said Jade, sulking.

'I'll play with you after dinner, OK?' I said.

She smiled.

I took all my presents to my room. I got DVDs, CDs, computer games, and some nasty brown socks and slippers from Auntie Kelly.

'Can I ring Dan?' I shouted downstairs.

'Yes!' said mum, from somewhere downstairs.

I dialled his number and waited. His mum answered and said a jolly Merry Christmas. She put Dan on the phone and I could hear his heavy breathing; something he had recently started to do.

'Merry Christmas!' I said. 'How's it going?'

'Merry Christmas. All good, thanks. All my family are here and some people from church, too. Got a right house full.'

'Good stuff.'

'What's it like at yours?'

'A bit quiet,' I said, lowering my voice. 'I'm playing with Jade most of the time. She got a toy kitchen so I've been pretending to eat plastic buns and bread all morning.'

He laughed and coughed.

'How're you feeling?' I said.

He cleared his throat and there was a long pause.

'I'm OK, just tired.'

'You'll be fine,' I said. 'I'll let you get back to your family.'

'OK, have a good day. Pop round soon, yeah?'

'Yup, I will,' I said. 'You have a good day, too.'

I put the phone down and looked out of my window. Mr Legna was in his garden, holding his steaming mug of tea. He was looking up at my room as if he was expecting me. I opened my window and said a Merry Christmas.

'And to you, Jamie,' he said, nodding. 'How's the glider?'

'Good,' I said. 'It's like new.'

He smiled and then chucked his used tea leaves on the grass.

15

Mum suggested we go for our Christmas walk. It was grandad who had started the tradition, way back when mum was about Jade's age. She said it was important to help keep good memories alive. The walk took us up Kaye Lane, through Almondbury Cemetery, through Round Wood, down Lumb Lane and back home. Grandad would always show me the little cottage on Kaye Lane that he grew up in.

He would tell me stories about what he and his friends got up to during the war. They played hide and seek and went looking for birds' nests. They camped out in the cemetery and told one another ghost stories. They played Cowboys and Indians and built dens in the woods. They pretended to be soldiers, using twigs for guns, and they would do 'Ip Dip Doo' to see who had to be the bad guys.

At the cemetery, he would always put flowers on nan's grave. He said that when his time came he wanted to be buried next to her. Mum would tell him to be quiet and to stop talking about such things. He just used to laugh, though, and tell her not to worry.

'Are you two ready?' said mum, looking at herself in the mirror above the fireplace. She was wearing her new dark green duffle coat that dad had bought her. 'What do you think?' she said, giving us a twirl.

Jade and I smiled.

'It's nice,' I said.

'Can *I* wear it sometime?' said Jade.

'You blummin' can't,' said mum, laughing.

Jade put some plastic buns in her oven. She said they would be ready for us when we got back.

'Put the oven on low,' said mum. 'You don't want them burning.'

I suppressed a smile as Jade rushed over to her kitchen and pretended to turn the temperature down.

'Is dad coming?' I said.

'I hope so,' said mum.

She went into the dining room where dad was reading the manual for his new watch. I heard her ask him if he was coming. There was a pause and she quietly said thank you.

'Come on, you two! Chop, chop!' she called from the kitchen. She was taking a bunch of flowers out of a vase when we walked in. She smelled them and smiled.

'What are those for?' I said.

'Your nan and grandad,' she said.

We put our coats, gloves and hats on and set off.

'Beautiful day,' said mum, taking a deep breath.

Jade copied her.

It felt like we were walking through a ghost town; either people were busy eating their Christmas dinner or they'd gone away to visit family and friends. We passed several dog walkers but that was it. Even the roads were empty. Dad was quiet, only speaking to tell Jade to keep hold of his hand. I walked alongside mum who seemed to be in her own world. I imagined grandad walking with us, telling me his stories, his adventures.

We got to the cemetery and found his and nan's headstones. Both were in the shadow of a large sycamore and were covered in dead leaves, flowers, gifts and ornaments. Mum said she didn't know who brought most of the stuff. On grandad's I spotted the small ornament that we got him for his eightieth birthday. It was an old man sitting in a chair on a pile of books. On the book spines it said, 'The World's Greatest Grandad'. There was his favourite blue mug, too, which was filled with dirty rainwater, drowned bugs and bits of bark.

Mum collected all the dead flowers and replaced them with the new ones. She got a tissue from her sleeve and wiped her eyes and nose.

I looked around and noticed several people visiting different graves. There was a man holding a baby. He was pointing to a headstone, trying to get the baby to look at it, then he kissed the baby's head. There was a family huddled together. All of them had their arms on one another's shoulders.

I wondered where Dan would be buried and what his grave and headstone would look like. I squeezed my eyes shut to try and get rid of the thoughts.

'You OK, love?' said mum.

I nodded.

There was a small robin singing in the tree. It looked to be staring right at me. It flew off and landed on a headstone alongside the path.

'Come on, guys, let's go,' said mum, 'before we all catch a cold.'

We started down the path and as soon as we got to the robin it flew off again. The headstone it had been perched on was ancient and the inscriptions on it were barely readable. Mum saw me trying to read it. She bent down next to me and squinted on the engravings.

'Thomas Edward,' she said. '1795 to 1808, I think. Very old, but very young.'

I couldn't speak

'They didn't live as long back then,' she said. 'Not like we do now.'

'Where do we go, mum?' I said, not taking my eyes off the headstone.

She thought for a moment.

'We go to a place where there's no more pain.'

'What else? Is there something else when we die? What about heaven?'

She picked up a dead leaf and held it between her gloved fingers. It was all brown and soggy.

'When your nan got ill,' she said, 'she told me never to worry. She said she would be watching over us.'

'From heaven?'

Mum giggled a little. 'Well I hope so; you can't watch over someone if you're below them.'

She gently returned the leaf to the ground and continued. 'The thing about your nan is that she'd never told a lie in her life. So I believe she's somewhere close, watching us, protecting us, guiding us.'

'And grandad?'

'He'll be there,' she said, looking up. 'You don't think he would leave you, do you? You were his favourite; the first boy in the family.'

'I still talk to him,' I said. 'He never talks back, though.'

'Keep trying, love. It won't do you - or him - any harm.'

'I miss him.'

'So do I, love. So do I.'

'You coming or what?' said dad.

16

I didn't want to go back to school at all. Mum thought it would do me the world of good to see my friends again, but I said they weren't my real friends. People like Luke, Princey, and Murphy used to be my friends, but not anymore.

We used to all hang out and play football, up at the school field. One day, after school, Murphy threw a stone straight through the science lab window. He ran away, laughing, followed by Princey and Luke. The caretaker appeared at the hole in the window and saw me, Teddy and Dan, standing there. He reported us to the headmaster, Mr Nolan. The next day, the three of us got detentions and had to stay behind after school. Mum and dad said they were disappointed in me. I told them I hadn't done anything. I even told them who it was but I still got grounded for two weeks.

On the way to school, I walked past Mr Legna's house. He was standing at the window, holding his mug of tea, like usual. I waved and he grinned. I got to Teddy's house and knocked. There was no answer. I knocked harder. Teddy's head appeared at the landing window.

'Two mins.'

I breathed out slowly, watching my breath disappear. The door opened and I heard Teddy's dad shout from somewhere in the house, 'Have a good day!'

'Can't be bothered with this,' said Teddy, locking the door. 'I hate going back after Christmas; I'll have forgotten how to write!'

We walked past Dan's house. The living room curtains were still pulled shut. I wished he was coming with us and Teddy agreed.

'I'm dreading what people are going to say,' I said.

'What do you mean?'

'Well, people are going to be asking how Dan is. I imagine everyone'll know.'

'Maybe not,' he said.

'Dan's mum will have rung the school and told them what's happening. The teachers need to know. If people don't know by now, they will soon.'

We got to school and went to our separate Form Rooms. We all sat in silence as Mrs Alard did the register.

'You missed out Dan, Miss,' said Sara.

'I *know*, Sara,' said Miss, not looking up.

She finished the register and told us she had some sad news. My heart started to flutter. I didn't know why because it was about Dan, not me, and I even knew what she was going to say. She said she'd been told that morning that Dan had been diagnosed with cancer. She told everyone he'd be starting radiotherapy treatment soon, to try and shrink it. She said we should all send our best wishes and pray that he gets better. The silence in the room was awful. Nikki and Leanne started sniffling. Miss took her glasses off and wiped her eyes.

'Did you know?' whispered Princey from behind me.

'Yeah.'

'Shit, that's bad.'

The bell rang for the first lesson and Mrs Alard asked me to stay behind. She was a small, round lady with kind eyes. Her hair was black with silver strands in it and was always tied up at the back. When she wasn't chewing the tip of her glasses, they hung around her chunky neck on some red string.

'I know you knew about Dan before any of us,' she said, sitting back in her chair. She picked up a pen and began to click it, on, off, on, off. 'I know it must be tough for you, so if you need anything, just ask.'

'Thanks, Miss.'

'That poor boy,' she said. 'He's a bright lad. So much potential. I'll go round and see him some time. Do you think that would be OK?' She took her glasses off and began nibbling the tip.

'I think so. He'll be getting a lot of visitors; people from church, and all that. I'd ring before you go.'

She nodded.

'I think I'll buy a big card for the whole class to sign. What do you think?'

'Yeah, he'll like that.'

She smiled and continued to nibble her glasses and click her pen, on, off, on off, on, off.

*

At break time, Luke, Princey and Murphy were playing football in the field. They tried hitting me with the ball. They laughed, even though they missed. Murphy ran to get it and called me a loser. He pretended to throw it in my face and they all howled when I flinched. Teddy came running behind me.

'Here comes another pussy!' said Luke.

Teddy gave him the finger.

'Dickheads,' said Teddy. 'Did Mrs Alard mention Dan?'

I nodded.

'What did she say?'

'Nothing much, just that we should all pray that he gets better. She said she's going round to see him some time.'

'I never really liked her, you know, but maybe she's not that bad.'

'She's always been fine with me. She cried when she told everyone the news.'

'Really?' he said, eyebrows raised.

We sat on the bench, next to the empty tennis courts.

'Feels weird without Dan,' he said.

'I know.'

'Do you think he'll ever come back to school?'

'I don't know,' I said. 'I've no idea.'

The ball suddenly cracked Teddy on the back of the head.

'Nobheads!' he yelled, rubbing his head. He booted the ball down the field, away from them. 'Get it yourself!'

17

We went to see Dan every other day before his treatment started. We watched DVDs in his room and played on his Playstation, just like we always had done. We talked about stuff that seemed important, but looking back it was nonsense; it was the good kind of nonsense, though, the kind that made us laugh. The one thing we didn't talk about was his illness. That was the elephant in the room that we all chose to ignore. Sometimes I even forgot about it and I'm sure Teddy did, too. I don't know about Dan, though.

When he started his treatment, Teddy told me he didn't want to go and see him anymore. He said he hated to see him getting worse and knew that the treatment would speed it up. He'd seen it on TV; people losing their hair and going thin.

'But it's Dan,' I said. 'He's our friend. I know if I was ill then I'd want you guys to come and visit.'

He didn't reply.

'Imagine how hard it is for Dan,' I added.

Teddy gave in after that.

Dan's dad answered the door on our next visit. He was smiling and cheerful, as always.

'Come on in, boys,' he said. He shook both our hands and patted us both on the shoulder.

There were people laughing in the living room; voices I didn't recognise.

'Has he already got visitors?' I said.

'Just some of the lads from church,' he said. 'It's OK, though, it won't be too crowded. Go on in.'

Dan was sitting on the sofa. There were two boys sat at either side of him and one on the chair, opposite. They looked like they were in Year Ten, at least. Dan's dad followed us in and introduced us. We sat on the floor. Teddy wanted to leave, I could tell.

'Right,' said the oldest looking one, 'we better get going.'

They said it was nice to meet us and for us to look after Dan. We said we would. Dan thanked them for coming and said he would see them soon. His dad saw them out to save Dan getting up.

I sat in the warm chair opposite Dan and Teddy sat next to him.

'How you feeling?' said Teddy.

'Tired.'

'Is it the treatment?' I said.

Dan nodded.

'I'm looking forward to the weekends where I don't have to have it,' he said. 'Do you two want a drink?'

'I'm OK, thanks,' I said.

'I'm fine,' said Teddy. 'How do you feel then, you know, after the treatment?'

Dan took a deep breath and shut his eyes.

I watched his chest rise and fall under his favourite white t-shirt. It said FUBU on it in blue. His eyes remained shut for a few moments and Teddy looked at me.

'Do you want us to go, man?' I said.

Dan opened his eyes as if he was just waking up.

'No, no,' he said. 'I'm just a bit... tired.' He leaned forward and tried to reach his pillow from behind him.

'You want it moving?' I said.

'Please.'

I moved it further up. He leaned back and gave out a sigh like an old man.

'The radiotherapy,' he said. 'God. I know I've only had two doses of it but-'

'We can go so you can to rest,' I said.

'No, no, stay,' he said. 'How's... school?'

'Crap,' said Teddy.

Dan smiled.

'I miss it, you know.'

'Really? Bloody'ell, I wouldn't.'

'Mrs Alard said she's going to visit you some time,' I said.

Dan smiled and coughed. He struggled to get comfy.

'Loads of people have been asking how you are,' I said.

'Have they?'

He shut his eyes again and took another slow deep breath.

His mum came into the room. She smiled and gave us both a hug.

'It's nice to see you boys,' she said.

She looked at Dan and saw his closed eyes.

'The treatment's making him sleepy,' she said.

Teddy and I nodded.

'He's getting better, though,' she said, bending down and stroking his hand. 'God won't take him away from us so soon. We're all praying for him.'

'I think we should go,' said Teddy.

'Yeah, we'll let him rest,' I said.

Dan opened his eyes and said he would see us soon.

I held his hand to do our handshake, but it was limp. His mum looked at me, concerned, then smiled.

18

Four weeks had passed by the time I got to go to the hospital with Dan. My mum rang school and asked if it was OK. She said she would've still let me go even if they had said no.

Dan's mum rang me the night before. She told me what to expect and for me to be at their house for ten o'clock. She said she was going with us, so I wasn't to worry. She told me to bring a drink and a snack. She asked me if I could ask Teddy and see if he wanted to come, too, as there would be room in the taxi. I phoned Teddy straight away but he said he didn't want to. He said he didn't want to have time off school. He was lying, though, I could tell.

Dan had deteriorated a lot. We had to ask him several times to repeat what he had said because his voice was down to a mumble and a croak. He found it hilarious when we thought he was saying something completely different to what he actually meant. His walking stick had been replaced by a frame, with two wheels at the front for extra stability. If he didn't use that he had to be supported, step by step, by someone strong and sturdy; usually his dad or a friend from church.

He constantly had visitors, so I only saw him once a week. Teddy really hated going. He got upset on a few occasions and had to leave. Dan told his mum and dad that he didn't want anybody around him who would just sit there and cry. He knew how he looked and he knew he was getting worse. I told Teddy and he thought it would be best if he stopped going.

Nurses came every Monday, Wednesday and Friday to check up on him and to help his mum and dad with anything they needed. His mum always said how grateful she was for their help and gave them iced buns and cream cakes to take home.

It was absolutely chucking it down on the morning I was going to hospital with Dan. Mum said it woke her up at about six o'clock and she couldn't get back to sleep because of it. I ran all the way to Dan's and his mum told me to get in quickly.

'Jamie's here!' she shouted to Dan.

I heard him mumble something.

'No Teddy?' she said.

'He didn't want to take time off school.'

'OK.' She smiled gently.

Dan was sitting at the dining room table, just finishing off his breakfast. He gave me a slow motion thumbs-up when he saw me.

'Pissing it down, eh?' he mumbled, looking at how drenched I was.

'Just a bit.'

His mum came in and took away his empty bowl. She wiped his mouth with a piece of kitchen roll. Dan saw me watching so I looked away.

'The Met Office has given a weather warning for today,' said his mum.

'Really?' I said.

'Yeah, floods. North-east and west. So that's where we are now *and* where we're going. Never mind, we'll be fine.'

She went to the kitchen, took a swig of her tea and poured the rest down the sink.

'The minibus should be here in about five minutes,' she said. 'I'll just go upstairs and dig out my raincoat.'

It was the first proper uncomfortable silence between Dan and I. All I could hear was Dan's forced breathing and the heavy rain. I was going to tell him what Jade had been saying in her sleep, but I didn't want to freak him out.

He glanced over at me. He looked tired and worn out. His blinks were long and he kept on licking his dry lips. He smiled.

'It's hard to be like normal, eh?' he mumbled.

He was right. Everything had changed.

'Listen,' he said. 'I want to tell you something.'

I edged my chair forward to hear him better.

'Last night, or early this morning... I can't remember... it was still dark, though. People... there were... there were some people.'

'From church?'

He shook his head and smiled as if I was way off. He licked his lips and was just about to start talking again, when someone knocked on the front door.

His mum came running down the stairs. She opened the door and greeted the minibus driver. 'Quick. Quick,' she said. 'Get in.'

Dan put his hand on mine and told me he would tell me later.

'This is Jamie,' said his mum, and the driver shook my hand.

'Nice to meet you, lad,' he said. 'I'm Steve.'

He was thin and walked with a limp. His glasses were massive and made his eyes look like they were going to pop out of his head. His hair was short and flattened by the rain, so I could see his red scalp.

'Jamie'll be coming with us today,' said Dan's mum. 'Just for that little extra support.'

'Not a problem,' said Steve. 'There's plenty of room. Mr Turner's the only other patient I'm taking today. He'll probably be asleep most of the time, anyway, so we'll just have to be quiet.'

'I'm sure we can manage that, can't we boys?' she said.

She helped Dan stand up and put his coat on. She put his woolly hat on for him and pulled his hood up.

'You ready, pal?' said Steve to Dan.

Dan put his arm around him and they shuffled to the door. Steve counted: three, two, one, and then they set off to the minibus as fast as they could. I ran ahead and opened the sliding door. I climbed in and sat down. Dan's mum sat facing me. Steve sat Dan to my right, closest to the sliding door. Mr Turner was strapped in behind Dan's mum, facing the front. He was really old. His head was right back as if he was looking up and his eyes were shut, although his mouth was wide open. Steve fastened Dan's seatbelt and whispered to me that Mr Turner was catching flies.

Steve found Dan a wheelchair as soon as we got to the hospital. He said he would be waiting for us at the main entrance in an hour.

'You want to push him?' said Dan's mum.

I said yes, but I didn't really want to.

It felt strange pushing my friend in a wheelchair. I looked down and watched his head lowering as if he was falling asleep. He had changed so much in a few weeks that I was trying to remember what he used to look like. People stared at him and then at me.

We went to the waiting room and found a seat. People of all ages were there. There was a big lady on her mobile phone, complaining she had been waiting for ten minutes. There was an old bald man, wearing a grey suit. He was flicking through the pages of a National Geographic magazine. There was an old Indian lady sitting by herself, looking out through the window blinds. Dan's mum reached into her bag and pulled out two small oranges. She gave me one and I put it in my pocket for later. She peeled the other and began feeding Dan. She said it would give him energy. He chewed as if he didn't have any teeth. We waited for about fifteen minutes before a nurse came in with a clipboard. She looked down at it and then at all the people sat waiting.

'Daniel Cox,' she shouted with a smile.

His mum put her hand up like we do in lessons.

'Are you OK to wait here, Jamie?' she said.

I nodded.

'It doesn't take long.'

'OK. I'll look at a magazine or something.'

She wheeled Dan down the corridor and entered a room on the right.

I scanned the magazine rack and got a National Geographic. The front cover was a picture of a snake on top of a golden sand dune. You could see the winding trail it had made to get there. There was one fluffy cloud in a blue sky, eclipsing the entire sun.

An old man lowered himself into the seat next to me. We smiled at one another.

I got a bottle of water out of my bag and had a sip. I peeled my orange and offered him a piece.

The young woman who was sat two seats away turned to me and said no thanks, making me frown.

The old man chuckled.

I ripped off a segment and put it in my mouth; juicy and tangy.

'I'm Jamie,' I said.

'Nice to meet you, Jamie,' he said. 'I'm Fred.'

'What you in here for?' I said.

'Supporting my better half,' he said, and pointed to the old lady, sitting on the other side of me. I hadn't even seen her. She was stroking a fluffy heart on her key ring.

'She looks nervous,' I whispered.

Fred nodded. 'She always is when she has an appointment. She expects the worst all the time. I keep telling her I'm always here and that there's no need to worry. She doesn't listen, though.'

She carried on stroking the heart and looking up at the clock.

'We're always in good hands, Jamie,' said Fred. 'Remember that.'

The same nurse came in with her clipboard and shouted another name, but I didn't hear it. Fred's wife slowly got up, grabbed her coat from the back of the chair and smiled at me.

'He's right,' I said. 'You should listen to him.'

'Who, sweetheart?' she said.

'Your husband.'

She glared at me as if she was frightened. She kept on looking back at me as she followed the nurse down the corridor.

Fred laughed and said it was a pleasure talking to me. He follow his wife into the room on the left.

*

Dan and his mum came back ten minutes later. She asked if I was OK. I told her about Fred and how he was there to support his wife.

'Bless you,' she said. 'At least you weren't by yourself.'

Dan looked even more drained than before. His eyes were half shut and his head kept on dipping forward.

We walked down the corridor, past the room on the left. I stood on my tiptoes and had a look through the small window in the door. Fred's wife was sat down. She had something wrapped tightly around her arm and the nurse was looking at a computer screen. Fred was nowhere to be seen.

19

Dan slept all the way home. He only stirred when Steve shouted and swore, because another driver went through a red light, nearly hitting us.

'We could do without that,' said Dan's mum, putting her hand over her heart and taking a breath of relief.

I listened to the rain as it pelted the minibus. It sounded like popcorn in the microwave. We drove past flooded fields and went through massive puddles. There was one field that had an island of grass sticking up out of the water. On it was a little lamb not knowing what to do. Dan's mum said she felt sorry for the farmers and their animals in weather like this. She said she had been praying for them. The clouds parted and a beam of golden light shone down on the field next to us. She said it was the light of God. She said that all prayers are answered eventually, and if we ask for help it will be given to us. She said we need to be quiet inside to hear God's wisdom. Dan opened his eyes, looked around, and slowly shut them again. I pointed out a rainbow in the distance. She told me to make a wish.

*

When we got back, Steve lowered Dan onto the sofa.

'Thanks,' Dan mumbled.

'No worries, buddy,' said Steve. 'I'll see you tomorrow.'

He drove off with some cream cakes and iced buns. Dan's mum asked if I wanted to stay for lunch. I said I would. She put the TV on, switched over to the Comedy Channel, turned the volume down and went into the kitchen. Dan opened his eyes and looked over at me.

'Thanks, man,' he mumbled.

'It's OK.'

He sat up and struggled to get himself comfortable. He asked me if I could put a cushion behind him, to help him sit up better.

He coughed and licked his lips.

I asked him what he wanted to tell me before we went to the hospital.

He smiled.

'I woke up... and they were there.'

'Who?' I said.

'Angels. Four of them.'

I was speechless.

'I wasn't dreaming,' he said. 'I opened my eyes... there they were. They were sat at the end of my bed. My whole room... was lit up.'

'Lit up?'

He swallowed and nodded slowly.

'Light. The brightest... I've... I've ever seen. Brighter than the sun... but it didn't hurt my eyes. It was so... so warm.'

He shut his eyes.

'Have you told your mum?' I said.

He shook his head. 'Don't want to worry her. This is between me... and you, yeah? I don't even want you... telling Teddy.'

'What do you think they wanted?'

'I don't know. They didn't say anything. I just felt... great. Free. I felt like everything's just going to be fine.'

'Weren't you scared?'

He shook his head. He spluttered and ran his dry tongue over his cracked lips.

'They were angels, Jamie. Angels.'

20

It had stopped raining by the time I left. Dan's mum gave me a hug and thanked me for coming. On the way home I knocked on Teddy's door. His mum answered. She was wearing a yellow apron that had on it an outline of a sun.

'Hello, Jimmy, love,' she said. 'Come on in. He's just got back from school.'

It never mattered what she was cooking; their house always smelt the same. It was a mixture of old people, soap and meat.

'I'm just making leek roly-poly with steak,' she said. 'It's his dad's favourite. It was the first meal I made him, way back in 1945. I was living with my mum back then. Blind, she was. It was a vaccine that did it. I was three when I started looking after her, you know. I paid the coalman and helped her get the bus to town and back; a lot of responsibility for a little'un. I bet you can't show me anyone your age with responsibilities like that.'

Teddy's dad walked in and told her to shut her pie hole. He told me to escape and go on upstairs to Teddy's room.

Teddy was sitting on his bed in his school uniform, reading a computer games magazine.

'Grab a seat,' he said, pointing to his black desk chair.

His walls were dotted with the odd random poster. There was one that was full of different dinosaurs and another that was a bird's eye view of a city at night. There were wrestling figures on his window sill; they were in a toy ring as if a fight had been paused.

'How're you?' he said, not looking up from his magazine.

'I'm OK. Your mum called me Jimmy again.'

'Told you she's losing it.'

'How was school?' I said.

He shrugged. 'Same.'

'Why didn't you come today?'

'You know why.'

His dad was whistling downstairs and his mum yelled at him to stop.

'So, how was it then?' he said.

'OK, I guess.'

'How's he doing?'

'Super tired. His voice is going. He finds it harder to walk, too.'

He flicked the pages of the magazine. It was obvious that he was just looking at the pictures.

'Why don't you come to Dan's with me next time?' I said. 'It'll be next Tuesday, I think.'

I went and picked up a wrestling figure and pulled the lever on its back, making it do a karate chop.

'I don't want to.'

'Why not?'

'You *know* why not, man! I don't like to see him like that.'

'So you're not going to visit him again?'

'*Course* I will.'

'When?'

'I don't *know*!'

'Come on, Teddy, he's your friend. If it was you who was ill, Dan wouldn't think twice about coming to visit. We've known each other since we were five.'

'Ex*actly*! I *hate* to see him like that. I know I should go and see him, and I feel bad not doing, but I'm not like you; I can't just act as if everything's normal.'

He whipped over the pages as if they were burning his fingers.

'Maybe Luke's right,' I said. 'Maybe you are a pussy.'

He threw the magazine on the floor and stormed out of the room.

I heard him lock the bathroom door. His dad came upstairs and asked what all the shouting and banging was for.

'A sensitive one is that,' he said, sitting on Teddy's bed. 'He's not taking this whole Dan business too well.'

'I just want him to come and visit,' I said. 'I don't know how he can't; he's one of his best friends.'

'The Three Amigos,' he said, chuckling. 'That's what we call you.'

I picked up the magazine and put it on Teddy's desk.

'Listen, my lad,' he said, 'people deal with this kind of thing in different ways. Teddy's scared, that's all.'

'I am, too.'

'Yes, but you're stronger than he is. You have to let him be. You can't force someone to change. When the time's right for Teddy, he'll visit Dan.'

I nodded.

'I better go,' I said.

I knocked on the bathroom door. I could hear Teddy sniffling.

'Sorry, man,' I said. 'I'll see you soon, yeah?'

He didn't answer, though.

'He'll be fine,' his dad whispered.

The smell of leek roly-poly hit me as I headed downstairs.

'Smells nice,' I said.

'It was the first meal she ever made me,' he said. 'Way back in forty-six.'

'Forty-five,' said Teddy's mum, washing her hands at the kitchen sink.

'Forty-six, dear,' he said, rolling his eyes.

'Forty-five, you daft beggar,' she said.

He ignored her.

21

When I got home there was a note on the kitchen worktop, next to a packet of fizzy snakes.

>JAMIE, GONE TO THE PONY PARK.
>WON'T BE LONG.
>COME UP IF YOU LIKE.
>THESE SWEETS ARE YOURS.
>M & J xx

I opened the fizzy snakes and made my way to the park. I could see Jade on the swings straight away. Her deep red coat stood out a mile. When she saw me, she shouted my name.

'So how was it?' said mum, standing aside so Jade didn't swing and hit her.

'OK,' I said.

'Dan better yet?' said Jade.

Mum gave her a huge push. She screamed with excitement.

'No, not yet,' I said.

'Can I have a snake?' she said.

'What do you say, Jade?' said mum.

'Please?'

'That's better.'

Mum held onto the swing and slowed her down. I pulled out a red and green snake and made a hissing noise, and pretended it was going to get her. She laughed and took it off me and bit its head off. She scrunched up her face and we laughed.

'Fizzy, eh?' I said.

She nodded, took another bite and pulled the same face again.

'So how's Dan?' said mum.

I told her how tired and weak he was and how he kept on licking his dry lips. I told her I pushed him in the wheelchair and how Steve swore when we nearly hit a car.

'What's swore?' said Jade.

'Never you mind,' said mum.

'Looks like it's going to rain again,' I said.

Mum looked up and around.

'I think you're right. I knew it wouldn't stay fine for long. Come on, Jade, we'd better get a move on before it starts.'

Jade held up her arms and I lifted her out of the swing. She walked in between us on the way home, holding our hands. We swung her over puddles and told her to jump on a count of three.

'One, two, *three*!' we all said together.

'Higher! Higher!' she said. 'I want to touch the clouds.'

*

We just got to the stop of our driveway when it started to rain.

'Run!' said Jade, laughing and running down to the back door.

I noticed Mr Legna watching us from his living room window. We waved at each other.

'Who you waving to?' said mum.

'Mr Legna.'

'Oh, really? I haven't seen him yet.' She took a couple of steps back and looked for him. 'Oh, he's gone. He could do with cutting his grass, his garden's a right tip.'

Mum put the kettle on even before she took off her coat.

'Can I have a bun?' said Jade, whilst taking off her pink and white trainers.

'What do you say?' said mum.

'Please?'

'There you go,' said mum, giving her two. 'One's for Jamie.'

We sat down in the living room and I clicked the fire on. The fake flames danced up a fake chimney. Jade turned the TV on and sat down in front of the fire. With her finger, she scooped out all the sweet cream from inside her bun.

'Can I just have a look at the news,' said mum, 'then you can watch whatever you want.'

It was showing how much damage the rain had caused. Streets had been turned into rivers. Cars were left abandoned with water gushing through the windows. It showed rescue teams helping people out of their homes. It showed inside shops, with packets of crisps and newspapers floating on top of brown water. Shop keepers were being interviewed, saying they had lost everything. They said it would take months and months to get things up and running again. Mum shook her head all the time, saying how devastating it all was. She said how lucky we were to live on high ground.

The next story was about a boy who had been found dead in his bedroom. He was fifteen. His Dad said it was a mystery. He said he went to wake him to go and play football. He said he thought he was joking at first because there was a smile on his face. But then he noticed he wasn't breathing. He tried to wake him but couldn't. He said he was fit and healthy and didn't show any signs of being unwell.

'How awful,' said mum. 'Poor soul.'

'So they don't know what happened to him?' I said.

Mum shook her head. 'Whatever he saw it made him smile.'

'An angel,' said Jade, throwing the last bit of bun into her mouth.

'Maybe love,' said mum. 'Maybe he saw an angel and it took him to heaven.'

Jade agreed.

22

Dad got home an hour late that night. Mum asked him where he had been. He said he had to show a new lad the ropes for the night shift and it took longer than he expected. She didn't say any more about it. He put his dinner in the microwave and began sifting through the post.

'Crap, crap, crap,' he said, ripping them up and throwing them in the bin. 'Jade in bed?'

I nodded.

'I went to the hospital with Dan today,' I said.

The microwave pinged. He tasted his food and put it back in for another minute.

'Oh yeah?' he said. 'How is he?'

'OK. He's finding it harder to talk and walk, though. The radiotherapy's taking a lot out of him.'

'I'm sure he'll be fine.'

He started looking at the sports pages of the newspaper.

The microwave pinged again and he bit into a chip. He burnt his tongue and swore. He sat down at the table and spread the newspaper in front of his plate.

'We'll talk later, OK?' he said.

I sat next to mum on the sofa. She looked at me but didn't say anything.

23

That night, I couldn't get to sleep. I couldn't hear mum and dad talking or arguing. I stared at the ceiling for what felt like hours. I could hear the wind and the rain banging against my window. I watched the monsters and the witches on my wall again, only this time I smiled at them. I thought about Dan and what he had said. Had he really seen angels at the end of his bed? I shut my eyes and tried to imagine what they must've looked like. In my mind they wore white robes that covered their feet, and they had long golden hair that shimmered and sparkled.

I got up and looked out onto the sodden street. I watched a raindrop dribble down my window. I followed it with my finger.

'Are you there, grandad?' I whispered.

No answer.

'Is Dan going to be OK?'

No answer.

'Is there such a thing as angels?'

Again, no answer.

I told him everything that had happened that day. I spoke to him as if he was in my room with me, sitting next to me, having a cup of tea in his favourite blue mug.

*

I was with Teddy and Dan. We were walking around Digley Reservoir. It was summer. I walked to the edge and looked in, trying to see the bottom of the murky water. To my side, I read a sign that said, "COLD WATER KILLS!" Suddenly Dan jumped in, followed by Teddy. They were splashing around and laughing. They shouted for me to jump in. I told them to get out, but they wouldn't listen. They were calling me a wimp and a chicken.

Someone came up from behind me and pushed me in. The water was freezing. It took my breath away. I looked up and saw Princey standing there. He wasn't laughing or doing anything; just standing there, glaring at me. I looked around for Dan and Teddy but I couldn't see them. Then they suddenly appeared behind Princey and they were dry. They yelled at me, asking me why I was in the water. They told me about the sign that said cold water kills.

I couldn't catch my breath. I could feel the icy water above my lips. Then it rose above my nose and my eyes. I started to choke. I went deeper and deeper and felt numb. I was surrounded by nothing but liquid charcoal.

Then a golden light appeared from beneath my feet. It sent beams of light shooting up, towards the surface. The light turned into a person. She had golden hair and crystal blue eyes. She was glowing. She smiled at me and I was no longer afraid. The cold water became warm and I felt safe. She carried me as if I was a baby.

'Jamie. Jamie!'

I opened my eyes and saw the outline of Jade standing next to my bed.

'What's up?' I said, trying to come round.

'They're in my room.'

I tried to focus on her but it was too dark.

'Who are?' I said, getting out of bed.

She held my hand and walked me to her room. She pointed to the corner, where her bears were piled up.

'Look,' she whispered.

I couldn't see anyone.

'Who is it? What do you see?'

She was silent. She looked around. She looked under her bed and under her sheets.

Looking confused, she said, 'Where've they gone?'

24

A few weeks later, mum asked me to go down to the petrol station to get some milk and a Sunday paper. Jade begged to come with me. Mum told her she had to get dressed first if she wanted to go. She ran upstairs and came down a few minutes later with her jumper on backwards. We laughed at her. Dad walked into the kitchen, yawning and rubbing his eyes. He put the kettle on and asked where the paper was.

'Just going to get one,' I said.

He disappeared into the living room and I could suddenly hear the sports channel. Jade gave mum a hug and a kiss before we left. She ran into dad and gave him a kiss on the cheek, too. He told her to be careful and to hold my hand.

We got to the top of the drive and I looked back to see Mr Legna, standing at his window. He waved. I told Jade I wanted her to meet him. We went to his door but he opened it before we even had a chance to knock.

'Morning,' I said. 'This is my little sister.'

He smiled broadly and bent down to her.

'Hello, you must be Jade,' he said, shaking her hand.

She giggled and said hello.

'We're going down to the petrol station,' I said. 'Do you want anything?'

'I'm OK, lad,' he said. 'Thank you for the kind offer, though.'

We said good bye and set off.

'I like Mr Legna,' said Jade. 'He's my friend. I like his eyes.' She began to skip whilst holding my hand.

'Why do you like his eyes?' I said

'Coz they're like the big, blue sea.'

*

'I've met Mr Legna,' said Jade, as soon as we got home. Mum was standing at the kitchen sink, washing up. 'He's kind. He has blue eyes, like the sea. He's a nice old man.'

'I still haven't met him,' said mum, sounding a bit frustrated. 'It's been nearly four months. I really should go round and see him.'

'You should,' I said. 'He'd be happy to see you. He'll probably invite you for a cup of tea.'

'That's what your grandad used to do. He'd invite any old Tom, Dick or Harry in for a cuppa. He used to say there's no such thing as strangers, only friends you haven't met yet. Sometimes it took him over an hour just to go to the shop and get some milk. Not because he was a slow walker, but because he spoke to everyone. Your nan would go ballistic if she had his dinner ready. She used to say he could talk his mouth dry.'

I remembered walking up to the village with him once to collect his pension. Everybody we passed said hello to him. Most of them even knew his name.

Dad came in, holding an empty cereal bowl. He went and put it in the sink. Mum said thanks, sarcastically. He thanked me for getting the paper and sat down at the table to read it.

'Will you be seeing Dan or Teddy today?' said mum.

'Dan'll be at church - I don't know about Teddy.'

She stared at me.

'You and Teddy aren't the same as you used to be, are you?'

I shrugged.

'Try not to let what's happening to Dan affect your friendship with Teddy. You'll regret it, love. Honestly, you will.'

'He makes me mad, though,' I said. 'I can't remember the last time he went to see Dan.'

'I thought you'd already had this conversation with Teddy's dad. He told you: Teddy isn't as strong as you. You need your friends at a time like this. I'm telling you, love, don't lose him.'

25

After lunch, mum washed the dishes and I dried them. Her hands were covered in bubbles; each one contained a rainbow.

'Can I go round to Mr Legna's later?' I said.
'Why?'
'Just to see him. Maybe go for a walk.'
She washed a cup and rinsed it out.
'Will you be calling for Teddy?'
'I doubt it.'
'So it'll just be you and this Mr Legna?'
'Yes.'
She picked up the big roast dish and dunked it several times. Puddles of fat rose to the surface of the water.
'I'm not sure I'm happy with you hanging around with strangers, Jamie.'
'He's not a stranger, Mum, he's our neighbour. I've spoken to him loads. He fixed my glider just before Christmas, remember?'
She nodded.
'So can I?'
She thought for a while, dried her hands and put the kettle on.
'OK, but be careful.'

'Remember what grandad used to say,' I said. 'There's no such thing as strangers only frien-'
'Yeah, yeah. Be careful, though.'

26

I kissed mum and Jade on the cheek before I left. Dad was watching football whilst mum read a magazine. Jade was playing with her toy kitchen in front of the fire.

'Gosh, this oven's red hot,' she said. 'Jamie, do you want a bun before you go?'

She got a tray out of her oven and pretended it was hot. Mum smiled and told her she should've used oven gloves. Jade handed me a plastic bun and told me to be careful.

'Thank you,' I said. I made noises as if it was delicious whilst rubbing my stomach.

She looked pleased with herself.

'We might be going to the garden centre in a bit,' said mum, 'so we'll put the spare key underneath the plant pot, next to the back door. OK?'

I nodded.

Mum shouted for me to be careful just as I was leaving. The air was cold and fresh. The blue sky was smudged with thin strokes of white clouds.

I was just about to knock on Mr Legna's door when he opened it.

'Hello, lad,' he said, 'what can I do for you?'

'I wondered if you fancied going for a walk,' I said.

He said he would love to. I told him I could show him Quarry Hill where we all usually played in the summer.

'You might want a coat,' I said, as he locked his door.

'I'll be fine. Cough sweet?'

They were the same spicy ones as before. He was right, they were good in cold weather.

We set off up to Quarry Hill. I told him about the neighbours that I liked and disliked. He laughed when I told him about Mr Grumps, as he was known on the street, who called the police, just because we were playing tennis on the street. I showed Mr Legna the cars that me, Dan and Teddy had washed last summer for a bit of extra pocket money. Mrs Hammond was standing at her window, staring at us as we walked past. Mr Birthright was washing his car and he stopped and stared, too.

'People are weird around here,' I said.

Mr Legna laughed.

'Why's that?'

'Everybody stares.'

'Why do you think that is?'

I shrugged. 'I don't know. Maybe they've heard about my friend.'

'The one with the tumour?'

I nodded, but then remembered I had never mentioned that to him before.

'How did you know?'

'People talk, Jamie.'

'He was diagnosed just before Christmas,' I said. 'He's not doing too well. The treatment's draining him.'

He walked with his hands behind his back. He watched the birds in the trees as I spoke but I still felt as if every one of my words had his whole attention.

'We've been friends since we were five,' I continued. 'His mum says he'll be OK. He seems to be getting worse, though, I think. He can hardly walk or talk. He can't feed himself any more, and last week he lost the movement in his right arm. It's just like he's crumbling away, bit by bit. His mum says God won't take him away from us. She says we all need to pray for him and our prayers will be answered and then he'll get better.'

'Do you pray, Jamie?' He got another cough sweet out of the white paper bag.

I shook my head. 'I don't know how to.'

We went up Quarry Hill Road, then up the steep path that led us to the top of Quarry Hill. We looked across at Almondbury Village. I pointed in the direction of the Pony Park and Round Wood. I pointed out my school and Morton Green, where my grandad used to live before he died.

'He died of lung cancer last year,' I said. 'My nan died when I was two so I don't really remember her.'

'Do you miss your grandad?'

'A lot.'

I looked up at the clouds and took a deep breath. A kestrel was hovering close by, waiting patiently to swoop in on its pray.

'Look how it uses the wind to its advantage,' said Mr Legna. 'Stunning.'

I looked at his thin grey hair blowing in the wind. He reminded me so much of my grandad.

'It might sound silly,' I said, 'but I still talk to him.'

'Who? Your grandad?'

I nodded.

'That's not silly,' he said. 'In fact, it's perfectly normal.'

'Sometimes I can feel him, almost as if he's right next to me.'

'Again, Jamie, that's perfectly normal.'

He was quiet for a while. I could see him from the corner of my eye, staring at me with his blue eyes.

'Do you believe in souls, Jamie?'

I sat down, pulled up a clump of grass and blew it off my hand.

'I don't really know what one is,' I said.

He sat down next to me and got himself comfy.

'Your soul is the part of you that never dies,' he said. 'What you're feeling when you talk to your grandad is his soul, his spirit.'

I picked up a stone and threw it as far as I could.

'Why doesn't he answer then?'

'Because he knows that there's a chance of scaring you. Imagine if he suddenly appeared by your side and answered your questions.' He laughed. 'Can you imagine what you would do?'

'Yeah, maybe you're right,' I said, thinking about it.

'Jamie, he's waiting for the perfect time to communicate with you. Like when you're sleeping, for instance.'

'When I'm sleeping? But I'll be *asleep*!'

'Yes, but then you won't be *afraid*. You won't question it or judge it, either. You'll remember it when you wake up. You'll tell people and they'll say it was a dream but to you it will have felt different from a dream. It will have felt real. And that's because it will have been.'

'So what are you saying? My grandad isn't dead?'

'That's exactly what I'm saying.'

*

I was quiet. I kept on thinking about Dan and the angels. I wanted to tell Mr Legna all about it but I'd promised not to tell anyone. I wanted to tell him about Jade, too, and the weird things she sometimes came out with at night. Then I thought about my grandad because if he wasn't dead, then where was he?

'I don't know,' I said, 'I find all this hard to believe. Why can't I see my grandad if he's there?'

Mr Legna put his hand down on the grass for a moment. He slowly lifted up his open hand for me to see.

'Look,' he said. There was a small green caterpillar on his hand. It was curled up, pretending to be dead. 'I'll tell you something about this caterpillar.' He got close to it and smiled as if it was an old friend of his. 'He doesn't believe in butterflies.'

'What?' I frowned.

'This caterpillar doesn't believe in butterflies because he can't see them, just like you and souls. He has no idea that his destiny is to turn into a beautiful butterfly. He just thinks that he eats and eats. Then he goes into his little chrysalis to rest and that's the end of it. Job done.'

I watched the caterpillar, still playing dead.

'You can't see your grandad because you are this caterpillar and all you see are other caterpillars. But your grandad, well, he's somewhere spreading his beautiful wings; for it was his time to turn into an amazing butterfly.'

I could feel a lump in my throat and tears forming in my eyes. Mr Legna looked at me and smiled. He put his hand down on the grass. He blew on the caterpillar and it came alive, crawling onto a thick blade of grass.

'I still don't want Dan to die,' I said, wiping my eyes.

'He won't die, Jamie, nobody does. This is why life is truly magical. Life never ceases to be. When his time comes, you might think he has died but what has really happened?'

I sniffed and wiped my eyes and my nose on my sleeve.

'Jamie,' he said, putting his hand on my shoulder, 'what will have happened to Dan when his time comes?'

'He will have turned into a butterfly,' I said.

He patted me on the shoulder and turned his attention back to the hovering kestrel.

27

The following morning I called for Teddy to walk to school. There was no answer. I knocked harder and then his dad came to the door.

'Morning, Jamie,' he said. 'Teddy won't be long. He's a bit under the weather today.'

'Really? What's wrong with him?'

'Bad head. Sore throat.'

'My mum says there's a bug going round,' I said. 'A lot of people seem to be getting sick lately.'

He stared at me for a while.

'I want to show you something,' he said, finally.

He went inside and came back with a small book. He handed it to me with both hands. It was super old and tatty, almost as if it had been put in the washing machine by accident. Even the black leather cover was falling apart. In the top left-hand corner was a faded Union Jack. The top right-hand corner was hanging on by a few delicate threads.

'Be careful with it,' he said. 'It's very fragile. This was my father's Bible from the First World War.'

'Really?'

He nodded, proudly.

'Open the first page - gently, mind - and read what it says.'

I read aloud. 'During the Great War, this sacred book saved my life on the 29th July 1916.'

'You see where it's damaged?' he said, pointing. 'A bullet did that. It hit the bible and ricocheted off.'

'No way,' I said. 'He was lucky.'

'Very lucky. He was a changed man after that. He took great pleasure in the simplest of things. He would look at trees, birds and flowers for hours on end. I'll always remember him gazing up at the sky one day and saying that every cloud was a beautiful mystery. My mother, bless her, couldn't understand what had gotten into him. "This isn't the man I married" she used to say.' He laughed. 'Every morning he used to say thank you before getting out of bed. He told me once that his guardian angel was with him on that day, if you believe in that kind of thing.'

'You showing Jimmy that Bible again?' said Teddy's mum, walking into the kitchen.

'What do you mean? This is the first time I've blummin' shown him!'

'You showed him last time he came.'

'Bloody crackers, you are, woman,' he said. 'Bloody crackers. And his name's *Jamie* not *Jimmy*. Lord, give me *strength*.'

Teddy walked in. His eyes were heavy and his hair was all messy.

'I'm not coming today,' he groaned. 'Think I've got the flu... or something.'

'Yeah, you don't look good,' I said.

'Thanks.'

'I'll call for you tomorrow morning and see how you're doing.'

'I'll get him a hot toddy to drink,' said his dad. 'Then I'll send him to bed with a hot water bottle and he'll sweat it out.'

*

I walked past Dan's house and the curtains were closed as usual. I went up Mountfield Avenue and up the path to Flemminghouse Lane. Halfway up, I could smell cigarette smoke and could hear laughing and shouting. I knew it was Princey, Murphy and Luke. I took a left, passed the scout hut and through the church yard. I could see them at the top of the path, sharing a cigarette, passing it between them. They were sniggering and spitting and giving people on passing buses the finger. I crossed over the road as a bus came, trying my best to hide behind it. I managed to get to the path at the side of the vicarage, but it was too late.

'Oi! Pussy!' yelled Murphy.

They ran over the road and pushed me against the wall of the vicarage.

'You want some of this?' said Luke, blowing smoke in my face.

I turned away.

'Let me go, I'm going to be late.'

'Aww,' said Princey. 'Teacher's Pet's going to be late.'

'You make me *sick*,' said Murphy. He hawked next to my foot. He was the only one whose face was covered in red and yellow spots. 'Where's your pussy friend, *Ted*dy bear?'

'He's not well,' I said.

'Aww, he's not well,' said Princey. 'Has he broken a nail?'

They all laughed.

'What happened to you guys?' I said. 'You didn't used to be like this.'

'*Sh*' up!' said Murphy. 'Who the hell are *you*? Our dad? What shall we do with him, boys?'

'Burn him,' said Luke.

'Torture him,' said Princey.

Murphy went to grab my collar but I ducked and ran under Luke's arm. I ran as fast as I could towards the garages.

'*Get* him!' said Murphy.

My heart was racing. I could hear their feet kicking up dirt and gravel. They were getting closer and closer. I took a left, towards the empty garage. I dived straight through where the window used to be. I sat in complete darkness with my back against the wall. The floor was damp and covered in broken glass, dirt and grit. I held my breath. I could hear them breathing, swearing and laughing. They shouted my name and told me to come out, wherever I was. They started to punch and kick the garage doors. They shouted they were only messing and that they wouldn't hurt me. I heard a twig snap close by. Murphy's arm shot through the window, holding a lighter. He sparked the flame and looked inside. He looked directly at me and grinned.

'Over here!'

They jumped through the window, howling and gobbing. I couldn't see their faces. I struggled to get to my feet but one of them pushed me down.

'You didn't know we knew about your little *crap*py hideout, did you?' said Luke.

They crowed and slobbered.

Princey kicked my bag away. It disappeared into the abyss.

I drew away, shrinking into the corner.

'Shall we just finish him?' said Murphy. He shone his lighter under his chin, casting eerie shadows on his face.

'Yeah. Nobody'll find him in here,' said Luke.

I squeezed my eyes shut and waited for the first blow. I silently asked for help. I begged.

All of a sudden, the whole garage lit up with light. The three of them just vanished. I heard them shouting and screaming. They were saying they were sorry. I tried to see what was happening but all I could see was golden light. It was everywhere.

It disappeared as quickly as it came and the garage door opened. It took a while for my eyes to adjust, but when they did, I could make out the outline of a man. He came over to me and held out his hand.

'You OK, lad?'

Mr Legna! I couldn't believe it.

He helped me off the floor. There was no sign of Princey, Murphy or Luke anywhere.

'Where did they go?' I said. 'What happened?'

He said he was just walking past and heard lots of commotion going on inside one of the garages. When he opened the door, three lads came running out, then he saw me curled up in the corner.

'Maybe I should be asking *you* what happened,' he said.

'The garage,' I said, 'it was full of light.'

And he just smiled.

28

Mr Legna asked me if I was OK to go to school. He said he would walk with me if I wanted. I didn't want to go, though. I wanted to go and tell Dan what had just happened. I wanted to tell him that I believed him. I told Mr Legna I was OK. I thanked him and he set off back home, walking with his hands behind his back. When he was out of sight, I ran the long way to Dan's. I was shattered when I got there. His mum answered and she looked shocked to see me. She noticed I was sweating and out of breath and asked me if everything was OK.

'Yeah, everything's fine.'

'Why aren't you at school?'

I told her my mum had asked me to babysit Jade for an hour whilst she ran an errand. She came back early so I thought I'd see Dan.

She looked at my school bag, then at me and frowned, as if trying to suss me out.

I asked her how Dan was before she could ask me anymore awkward questions.

'He's still very tired,' she said, 'very weak. We've given him a small ball to squeeze to get some movement back in his right hand. He's still laughing, though; you know what he's like. The nurses love him.'

'Would it be OK if I went up?'

'I'm sure he'll be happy to see you, no matter how tired he is.'

I gently opened his bedroom door. His eyes were shut. He was lying on top of his covers, with his head slouched to the right. There were photos of his family and friends, stuck to the wall. There were nearly fifty Get Well Soon cards stuck on the back of his door; including the large one that Mrs Alard got everyone to sign. There was a prayer Blue-tacked to the ceiling. Relaxing music was playing in the background; acoustic guitars and flutes.

I ever so slightly lowered myself into the chair next to him. I watched his chest rise and fall. Occasionally he coughed. His hair was slowly growing back in patches. He was wearing his favourite white t-shirt and blue tracksuit bottoms; they seemed to be hanging off him. I watched his left eye twitching and remembered that's how it all started. There was a baby monitor next to him and then I remembered seeing an identical one in the kitchen. The small green ball that his mum had mentioned was resting next to his hip. I picked it up and squeezed it. It squeaked loudly like a dog's toy.

'Shit.'

Dan opened his eyes and laughed and spluttered. He tried to sit up and get himself comfortable.

'How long... you been here?' he mumbled.

'Just a few minutes. You OK?'

'Why aren't you... at school?'

'Can we turn the monitor off?' I whispered. I didn't want anybody listening to what I was about to say.

He turned it over with his left hand, so the speaker was facing down and smiled mischievously.

'What's up?' he murmured.

'You're never going to guess what just happened.'

I got closer to him and spoke quietly.

I told him everything, from Teddy having the flu, to seeing the three idiots smoking at the top of the path. I told him how they chased me to the garages.

'Did you go to the empty one?'

I nodded. 'I jumped through the bloody window!'

His laughing made him cough.

I told him how they found me. How it was pitch black and I couldn't see anything. I told him how I closed my eyes and begged for help.

Dan stared at me. 'Then what happened?'

I said how the garage had filled up with light - a golden light, just like he had described - and how I could hear the idiots screaming and crying, saying they were sorry.

'Then the light disappeared,' I said. 'As soon as that garage door opened, it vanished. And then my *neigh*bour walked in! He said he was walking past and heard the whole thing.'

Dan smiled and asked about my neighbour.

'He's just some old guy,' I said. 'Nice, though.'

'What's his name?'

'Mr Legna,' I said. 'I don't know his first name.'

Dan started to cough and choke. I stood up and patted him on his back. He wouldn't stop. I shouted for Dan's mum but she didn't come. I ran out of his room and shouted from the top of the stairs. She came barging through the kitchen door and up the stairs. She ran to Dan's side and started to slap him hard on his back. He wouldn't stop coughing. I watched, panicking.

'Why was the baby monitor face down?' she shouted. '*Why*? You should *never* turn the baby monitor over, Jamie! Go and ring for an ambulance. *Quick*!'

29

I watched as the ambulance sped away with Dan inside. I ran home and tried the door, but it was locked. I knocked several times and shouted for mum through the letter box. I sat on the doorstep, crying. I prayed that Dan wouldn't die. If he did it would've been because of me. I cried until I was exhausted.

'Are you OK?'

I looked up and Mr Legna was smiling sympathetically.

'I saw you running home,' he said, 'and I knew there wasn't anybody in.'

'Dan's been rushed to the hospital,' I said. 'I was telling him about what had happened to me in the garage and he started coughing and couldn't stop. His mum shouted at me for turning the baby monitor over. I only wanted to talk to him in private. They took him away... they put an oxygen mask over his nose and mouth and everything.'

I cried more until my breathing was shaking.

'Dan's going to be fine,' he said. 'He's in good hands.'

'I've been told that before,' I said, sniffling. I thought for a moment. 'It was the old man who

I met in the hospital... when I went with Dan for his treatment. Erm... Fr-'
'Fred?'
'Yes, how did you know?'
'You told me.'
'Did I?'

30

Seconds after Mr Legna had left, mum and Jade came home. I was still sitting on the doorstep when I heard Jade running down the driveway. She looked at me through the gate and smiled. She shouted my name and called to mum that I was home.

'What are you doing here?' said mum.

She was wearing the green duffle coat that she got for Christmas. She struggled to open the gate with all the bags of shopping. I opened the gate and took the bags off her so she could unlock the door.

'Have you been crying?' she said.

'Promise not to be mad,' I said, putting the shopping bags on the kitchen floor.

'What have you done?' she frowned.

'Nothing. Nothing. But, erm... instead of going to school I... I went to see Dan.'

'Why?'

'Well, Teddy has the flu so I ended up walking to school by myself. I bumped into the three idiots-'

'Who are?'

'Princey, Murphy and Luke.'

She nodded.

'They stopped me and held me up against the wall of the vicarage. They blew smoke in my face and said they were going to torture me.'

'They did *what*?' she said, filling the kettle.

'Honestly, they did.'

I wanted to tell her what happened next but I couldn't. I didn't want her to think I was making it up; that it was just my imagination. So I told her I ran to Dan's because I knew they wouldn't follow me there.

'I see,' she said. 'Shall I report the idiots to the school?'

'No. I don't think they'll be bothering me now.'

'OK. Now, explain the swollen eyes.'

I told her everything I had told Mr Legna and she sighed deeply. She looked to have tears in her eyes. She hugged me and kissed the side of my head.

'Don't blame yourself, love. Yes, you shouldn't have interfered with the baby monitor, but you know Dan's very poorly. His coughing fit could've happened at any time. It's not your fault. I'm sure he felt comforted to have you there.'

The kettle boiled and flicked itself off.

'Oh, and Jamie,' she said, 'let's keep this between me and you, OK? I don't think your dad would be too happy to find that you've taken time off school to go and see Dan.'

'OK. But what if the school calls?'

'It's OK. I'll take care of it.'

She told me to go and sit down and relax a bit. Jade was watching *Thomas the Tank Engine* whilst eating a chocolate bunny. The chocolate was all over her hands, around her mouth and even on her nose.

'Do you want some?' she said.

'Erm, no. I'm good, thanks.'

'Is Dan better?'

'Not yet.'

'He's in good hands, Jamie.'

'What?'

'He's in good hands.'

'What made you say that?'

She shrugged. 'Don't know.'

31

That night I rang Teddy and told him what had happened to Dan.

'Shit,' he said. 'Have you heard anything, you know, since it happened?'

'Nothing. I'll ring his mum and dad soon. My mum said they might keep him in overnight, to keep an eye on him.'

'I'm glad I wasn't there when he started coughing.' There was a long pause. 'Would I be able to see him, you know, seeing as though I have the flu?'

'Probably not,' I said. 'His mum said his immune system's low because of the treatment. They're scared of him getting an infection.'

'What would happen if he got an infection?'

'I don't know - make him worse, I guess.'

'Could it kill him?'

'I don't know.'

There was silence.

'Jamie, what if he doesn't come home?'

'I'm sure he will.'

'But what if he doesn't?'

'Then we visit him at the hospital.'

*

'Hello?' said Dan's dad over the phone.

'Hi, it's Jamie. How's Dan?'

'Hello there, son. Dan's out of hospital. He's just so tired, though. We're trying to let him rest as much as possible to get his strength up. That coughing fit seemed to take a lot out of him.'

'Glad to hear he's back home,' I said. 'Why's he coughing all the time?'

'It's all the phlegm, caused by the steroids. He took them to stop the swelling on his brain. It's just settling on his chest. He needs to cough it up and spit it out but he's getting too weak. So it builds up and up and then he ends up coughing like he did today. Jamie, his mum told me you rang for the ambulance.'

'Yeah.'

'Thank you. You're a God-send.'

I didn't feel like one.

'She also told me she lost her temper with you and wants you to know she's sorry. She didn't mean to snap at you like that.'

'The baby monitor shouldn't have been turned over, though.'

'It's water under the bridge now, son. It's OK.'

'Will I be able to pop round on Sunday?'

'I don't see why not. We won't be going to church, not with him like this. So we should be in all day.'

'So I'll come round about six-ish then?'

'OK, we'll see you then. Thanks for ringing... oh, and I'll tell Dan you've rung. All the best.'

*

Dad came home from work and put his dinner in the microwave. He started flicking through the post.

'Bill, crap, crap, and another bloody bill.' He tossed the envelopes on top of the microwave. 'Have you had a good day?'

'Dan had a coughing fit,' I said. 'I had to ring for an ambulance.'

'Really? Is he OK?'

I nodded but he didn't see me. He was looking at the sports pages in the newspaper.

'Yes,' I said.

'He'll be fine.'

'I don't think so. He's getting worse. He can't feed himself, or walk, or talk properly. His dad says he's got loads of phlegm on his chest that he needs to spit up.'

'Jamie, do you mind. I'm just about to eat.'

32

I was playing with Jade at the Pony Park. I was pushing her on the swings. She was shouting for me to push her higher and higher. She shouted that she wanted to go past the clouds and touch heaven. I pushed her as hard as I could. I could feel the breeze on my face as she whizzed past me. Then the swing came back down empty. Jade was gone. I ran around frantically, looking for her, shouting her name, trying to spot her red coat.

'Jade! Jade!'

I went into some woods and looked in the trees. I climbed up the tallest tree and looked over Almondbury Village. I jumped and floated back down like a feather.

There was something red swirling around in the blue sky. At first I thought it was a kite. It got closer and closer. Then I heard Jade laughing. The red thing was her.

'Jade, get down! What are you doing?'

She carried on laughing, spiralling down, getting closer and closer to me.

'Come on, Jamie, climb on, it's fun!'

It was only then that I realised she was on a cloud. She was riding it like a magic carpet.

'Get off it, Jade,' I said. 'It's dangerous.'
'It's not. It's fun!'
'You might fall off and hurt yourself.'
'I can't hurt myself,' she said, laughing. 'I'm in a dream!'

33

I went to see Dan two days later. I sat down next to him and the chair creaked. He opened his eyes. He said something but I didn't understand a single word of it. I put my ear close to his mouth and he said it again.

'Dad said you were... coming today.'

'I wanted to see how you were after the coughing fit.'

He licked his cracked lips and struggled to swallow. His breathing was heavy and he kept on taking short deep inhales.

'I'm... OK.'

'I feel bad.'

'Why?'

'If I hadn't have been talking to you, you wouldn't have started coughing.'

I had to get close again to understand him.

'It's... cool,' he said. 'It could've happened... at any time.'

He swallowed and took a deep breath.

'How's Teddy? I haven't seen... He hasn't been.'

'I know. He has the flu at the moment. I think he's scared he'll kill you if he comes.'

He laughed and broke into a cough.

'Teddy,' he said. 'Tell him... Hi.'

'I will.'

We didn't say anything for a while. I looked around his room at all the cards and we listened to the gentle music playing in the background. It was a combination of acoustic guitar and flute.

'Nice music,' I said.

'Mum's... It's relaxing.'

'Aren't you sleeping?'

'No... two hours... max'

He turned the baby monitor over, covering the speaker.

'I don't think that's a good idea, man,' I said.

'It's OK. Listen... the angels... they were at my bed again. We... we flew around, over fields... towns. I ran with them.'

He shut his eyes and smiled and caught his breath.

'Just relax,' I said.

'It felt so good... to run.'

He coughed violently. I reached for the baby monitor but he stopped my hand and said he was OK.

'Jamie...'

I got close to him. I could hear his heart beating. There were beads of sweat resting on his forehead.

'Soon... I'm going with them.'
'Where?'
'You know...' he said, looking straight at me.
Tears came to my eyes.
'Don't be upset. Death... dying... it's all safe.'
I looked down and wiped my eyes and my nose.
'What they've shown me... it's nothing... to be scared of.'
'I believe you,' I said.

*

We stayed in silence until his mum came into the room. She was humming and dancing. I quickly turned the baby monitor over before she could see. She got a cloth and wiped Dan's forehead.
'Gets warm in here, doesn't it, son?' she said.
She stroked his hand and kissed his forehead. She bent down and hugged me.
'We appreciate you coming, you know, Jamie.'
I smiled and hoped she wouldn't notice my red eyes.
'Don't you think he's getting better?' she said.
I nodded and wondered if she knew I was lying.

'He can nearly squeeze the ball and move his feet,' she said. 'He'll be up and running in no time, won't you, love?'

Dan looked at me, knowingly.

She walked over to the foot of the bed, crouched down and pulled out a board. It had all the letters of the alphabet on it and numbers from one to ten.

'Because the radiotherapy damaged his throat, some people find it hard to understand what he's saying, don't they love?'

Dan nodded.

'Especially when he gets visitors who haven't been with him since day one. To them, it's like he's speaking a foreign language. I think he likes to play games with them, though. He'll say something to make them get it wrong.'

We laughed. Dan coughed. She hit him on his back.

'He needs to get that phlegm up. It's those damn steroids that have caused it.'

I nodded.

'Where was I?' she said. 'Ah yes, the board. So whenever we don't understand him, he can spell out what he's saying.'

'It's a good job you can spell, Dan,' I said.

We laughed. Dan coughed.

He muttered something. Me and his mum looked at one another.

'Let's use the board!' she said, grinning.

She rested it on his knees.

He lifted his left arm and slowly moved his finger across the board, spelling: teddywouldbescrewed.

34

Teddy was standing at his bedroom window when I walked home. He was in his green dressing gown. His hair was fluffy as if he had just had a bath. He opened his window and asked how Dan was. I wanted to tell him what Dan had said, that he'll be going soon, but I couldn't.

'Just the same,' I said. 'How're you feeling?'
'Still a bit crap. Just had my Sunday bath.'
'I can tell, your hair's all fluffed up.'
He put his hand through it, looking embarrassed.
'Dan says Hi, by the way.'
He didn't say anything.
'When you get better, will you go round and see him?'
He nodded.
'I'll come with you,' I said. 'It'll be fine. He'll be happy to see you.'
'OK, yeah, when I get better. I don't want to give him the flu, that's all.'
'I told him you didn't want to kill him.'
'What did he say?'
'He laughed.'
Teddy smiled.

'Shut that window!' I heard his mum yell. 'You'll catch your death!'

Teddy rolled his eyes. 'I'll see you tomorrow morning'

'Oh, and Teddy, don't leave it too long before you see him.'

He frowned. 'Why?'

'Just, don't leave it long, that's all.'

35

Dad was watching the football when I walked in. Mum came downstairs moments later, shutting the door behind her, quietly.

'It's taken me ages to get her to sleep,' she whispered.

'It's all those sweets you give her,' said dad, taking a swig of Carling.

Mum sat down next to him, ignoring him. She picked up her glass of white wine and sat back, letting out a deep sigh.

'Dan OK?' she said.

I nodded and yawned.

'You should get an early night,' said dad.

Mum agreed with him.

She started flicking through the TV guide. Dad edged forward in his seat when a corner was given. He sat back, all disappointed when the keeper saved it.

'OK, I'm going to bed,' I said, getting to my feet.

They both said n-night in unison.

*

I brushed my teeth and crept into Jade's room. I knelt beside her bed. I watched her breathing. Her fingers twitched. Occasionally she smiled and her eyelids flickered, showing the white of her eyes. It was like she was in another world, somewhere completely different, yet so close.

'Where do we go when we die?' I whispered.

She grinned but didn't wake up.

'Do you know where we go, Jade? Is Dan going to be OK?'

No answer.

I got up and crept out of her room.

'Jamie,' she whispered.

I looked back. She was smiling, her eyes still shut.

'Soon,' she said. 'Dan will be OK soon.'

'Thank you,' I said.

36

The next morning, I called for Teddy. His mum answered the door and invited me in. She was frying bacon, sausages, eggs and black pudding, all in the same pan. Fat was spitting all over the unused hobs.

'Nothing like a good breakfast,' she said, pouring hot fat over the egg yolk. 'Keep you fit and healthy, this will.'

Teddy walked in with his school bag on his shoulder. He slammed it down on the floor and put his shoes on.

'Yeah, it'll keep Dad bloody fit, not me,' he said. 'I had to have bloody cereal.'

'Well, if you had gotten up earlier I could've made you some,' she said.

I watched as they bickered over breakfast.

'I never have bacon, eggs, sausages and black pudding for breakfast,' I said.

'See, Teddy,' she said, 'you don't know how lucky you are. During the war, we had rations. I can remember the first letter your dad ever sent me. He was on a ship sailing... somewhere.'

Teddy rolled his eyes as if he'd heard the tale a hundred times before.

She continued. 'They gave him something that he couldn't quite believe. It made him feel like a king. Do you know what it was?'

'White bread?' said Teddy.

'Yes!' she said. *White* bread. You ought to count your blessings. You never realise wh-'

'I'm off, mum,' he said. 'See you!' He shut the door behind us. 'Bloody barmy, that woman.'

The blinds were down in Dan's house. Two nurses pulled up in a white car, smiled at us and walked down the driveway.

We could hear voices when we got to the path. I knew who it was.

'Bloody hell,' said Teddy. 'Idiots. Let's go past the scout hut and through the churchyard.'

'No,' I said. 'Don't be scared of them. They won't do anything this time.'

All three of them stopped talking when they saw us. Teddy walked closely behind me. Princey smiled and nodded. We crossed over the road and headed up De Lacy Avenue.

'What the hell just happened?' said Teddy.

'I told you they wouldn't do anything'.

'Did Princey just smile?'

*

At lunch time, Teddy and I was sitting on a bench, eating out sandwiches, when Mrs Alard came and sat next to us. Teddy stopped chewing. He didn't know what to do at all.

'You don't mind, do you?' she said.

'No, no,' I said.

Teddy kept quiet.

'I've been wanting to ask you about Daniel,' she said. 'How is he? Is there any sign of improvement?'

I shook my head. 'I saw him last night. He's not doing too well, to be honest. His mum says she can see him getting better, but I can't.'

I could see the sadness in Mrs Alard's eyes. She looked into the distance and started to bite her thumbnail. Her glasses hung around her neck.

'He's OK, though,' I said. 'He's in good spirits. He isn't scared or anything. He's laughing a lot.'

She smiled. Her eyes filled up.

'He has this board,' I said, 'that has the alphabet on it and numbers from one to ten. People find it hard to understand him so he spells out what he's saying.'

She pulled out a tissue from the sleeve of her cream cardigan and wiped her eyes.

'I remember the first time I saw him,' she said, 'he helped me carry some my books to the

Staff Room; such a good natured boy. I was so pleased he was in my class. Do you two see him often?'

Teddy shook his head.

'Maybe once a week. Sometimes more,' I said.

I told her about Friday and how I had to phone for the ambulance. I told her about the phlegm on his chest and how he needs to cough it up.

'Poor soul,' she said. 'He was such an energetic little chap, so bright and cheerful all the time.'

'He still is,' I said, 'apart from the energetic bit.'

We sat in silence. We watched the Three Idiots playing football with some year sevens. Murphy slide tackled one and got the ball off him, leaving him on the floor, rubbing his mucked up knee. Murphy was just about to run and score when he stopped and turned around. He went over to the year seven, held out his hand and pulled him up. He patted him on the back and they carried on playing.

'They are a strange group of lads, those boys,' said Mrs Alard. 'I can never seem to figure them out.'

37

On the way home from school, I knocked on Mr Legna's door. He answered it straight away. He was wearing the same clothes he had on when I first met him: a brown and red woolly jumper that was frayed at the sleeves and brown cords, stained with blotches of white paint. I could hear the kettle boiling in the background.

'How're you?' I said.

'Couldn't be better, Jamie,' he said, his blue eyes sparkling like ice in the sun. 'Fancy a cup of tea?'

'OK,' I said. 'I can't stay long, though. Mum'll wonder where I am.'

I stepped into his dark kitchen.

'Which cup would you like?' He opened a cupboard and pointed to various mugs.

'The glass one, please.'

'Good choice,' he said. 'Take a seat.'

I sat down on the white wooden stool, in between the oven and the stove. I could feel the heat from the fire on my legs. I looked through the glass panel and watched the coal and wood burning away.

He opened a jar, stuck his nose in it and took a deep breath.

'Ahh! Heavenly,' he said.

He handed it to me and told me to have a smell. The jar was filled with what looked like small rolled up leaves. They smelt sweet and flowery.

'Jasmine,' he said. 'That's what that smell is. The tea leaves are flavoured with it.'

He put a few in my cup and poured boiling water over them.

'How's your friend?' he said.

I told him he was getting worse but was in good spirits. I said he wasn't scared and still laughed all the time.

'Can I tell you something?' I said.

He looked at me and smiled, waiting for me to speak.

'Dan's told me that he sees angels. He's told me they take him out of his body and he goes running and flying with them.'

'And do you believe him?'

'Yes, I do, but-'

I paused.

'The thing is, he told me that he's going to go with them soon.'

Mr Legna nodded. 'I see. And how do you feel about that?'

'Honestly? I was sad at first but now I'm OK. It feels weird saying this but... I think I'm happy for him.'

Mr Legna poured hot water over the leaves in his cup.

'You're no longer like the snowman who's scared of melting,' he said. 'You're starting to see that death and dying aren't things to be afraid of, but things to live with and make peace with. It's an adventure we all must go on. Your friend understands this; why do you think he's always happy?'

He handed me my cup of tea. I watched as the green leaves unravelled and sank to the bottom of the cup.

'Taste it,' he said. 'Tell me what you think.'

I took a sip. Then another.

'It's like drinking grass,' I said.

He howled with laughter.

38

A week later, the day before I was to take Teddy to go and see Dan, I got a phone call from Dan's dad. He sounded upset and in a hurry. He said Dan had been rushed to hospital because of breathing problems. He said he would keep me updated.

I could feel my heart drumming in my chest.

'Everything OK, love?' said mum, poking her head through the living room door.

'He's been rushed to hospital.'

She walked over and wrapped her arms around me.

'Will I be able to visit him?' I said.

'I'm sure your dad'll drive you up there if you ask him. You'll need to know what ward he's on.'

Jade walked in, wearing her pink spotted pyjamas. She was holding her favourite cuddly toy, Timmy the Tiger and covering her top lip with one of its ears. Without saying a word, she walked up to me and hugged me.

'Thanks, Jade,' I said.

She didn't say anything and tottered back into the living room.

'Can I ring Teddy?' I said.

Mum nodded and left me to it.

I told him everything and he cried. I told him Dan would be OK. I told him he was in good hands and that he wouldn't be in any pain.

'I should've gone to see him sooner,' he said. 'Bloody hell, I should've gone sooner.'

'You can see him when he gets out.'

'I've got a bad feeling, though, man. Maybe this time he won't get out. Maybe he won't come home.'

'Then we'll have to visit him in the hospital.'

'Bloody hell. *Bloody* hell! I *hate* hospitals. They give me the creeps. It's that damn smell and the long corridors.'

'I don't like them either. I had to visit my grandad there, remember?'

He sniffed.

'But this is Dan we're talking about now,' I said. 'Dan, our friend. He needs us. His dad's going to keep me informed. I'll ring you as soon as I hear anything, OK?'

'OK.'

'You going to be all right, yeah?'

'I'll be fine,' he said, sniffling.

*

Dad was watching the news.

'If Dan has to stay in hospital,' I said, 'could you take Teddy and me to visit him, please?'

He nodded. 'Yeah. After school.'

'Thanks.'

I stood in the doorway, not saying a word, but wanting to tell him everything.

'I'm going to bed,' I said.

'It's early for you isn't it?'

Mum came downstairs. 'Love, Jade wants to know if you can read her a story before bed.'

'Yeah, OK.'

'Don't have her laughing and getting all excited,' said dad. 'She'll never nod off then.'

Whilst heading upstairs, I could hear Jade talking to herself. When I opened her door she stopped suddenly and smiled at me.

'You OK?' I said.

She nodded.

'Who were you talking to?'

She shrugged her shoulders.

'What story do you want?'

She shrugged again. I started sifting through her books.

'No,' she said. 'Make one.'

'You want me to make up a story?'

She nodded and grinned. She pulled the covers up to her chin and shut her eyes, waiting for me to start.

'OK. You ready?' I said.

'Yup.'

'There was a caterpillar called Casey. And Casey didn't believe in butterflies.

'Every day he ate big leaves and got fatter and fatter. One day he started to wonder where his friend, Claudia the caterpillar, had gone. He shouted her name, "Claudia! Claudia!" but she didn't reply. He called out, "Where are you, Claudia? Why don't you answer me?" but again she didn't reply. Then one day, Franky the fly came buzzing along and heard Casey calling for his friend.

'"She's turned into a butterfly," he said, landing next to Casey on a big green leaf.

'"A butterfly?" said Casey. "Do you think I'm stupid? There's no such thing as butterflies."

'Franky the fly laughed at him and explained that Casey, too, would one day turn into a butterfly and fly away. "I saw your friend," said Franky. "She was flying around you, answering your questions, but you couldn't hear her because you're a caterpillar. She said she would be waiting for you when you turned into a butterfly."

'Casey still didn't believe Franky, but after eating lots of leaves, he went to sleep and woke up to find he had wings. He had a big stretch, and above him, flapping her beautiful wings, was Claudia. "There you are, Claudia!" shouted Casey.

"'I was here all along, Casey," she said, "but you couldn't see me."'

Jade was fast asleep. I kissed her on her forehead and tiptoed out.

39

Two days later, Dan's dad phoned and told me he had some bad news: Dan had caught pneumonia. He said Dan couldn't speak at all, so they'd come up with a new way to communicate with him.

'Dan now looks up for yes and down for no,' he said.

'Is that all he can do?' I said.

'Yes, I'm afraid so.'

He started to cry. 'I'm sorry.'

I waited. He blew his nose and got his breath back.

'They've told us to expect the worst. They haven't given him long. They've provided us with a single bed next to his, so we can stay overnight. His mum and I are taking it in turns.'

I didn't say anything.

'You can come and visit him tomorrow, if you like, Jamie? Don't feel like you have to, though. We'll understand if you don't want to. I'm sure Dan will, too.'

'No, no, I want to visit him. I'll come tomorrow, after school. Which ward is he on?'

'Ward Twelve. Thanks, Jamie.'

*

'I can't go,' said Teddy, the next day. We were walking home from school. 'I can't see him like that.'

'Please, Teddy, come on,' I said. 'Do it for Dan. He'll be glad to see you.'

'He can't *speak*, man! He looks up or down, that's *it*!'

I was silent.

'I can't go. I'm sorry.'

'So I'm going by myself then?'

His eyes were red and teary.

'My last memory of Dan is a fairly decent one. I don't want to remember him the way he is now.'

'OK,' I said. 'It's fine. I'll go by myself.'

He kicked a stone and it bounced off the kerb and hit a car. The alarm started going off.

'Shit,' he whispered.

40

Dad knocked on my bedroom door and asked if I was ready to go. He wanted to be back before the football started.

I ran downstairs and put my trainers on.

'Jamie!' called mum.

I poked my head around the living room door.

'You sure you don't want me to come?' she said.

'It's OK,' I said. 'I'll be fine.'

'Dan'll be better soon,' said Jade, playing with her toy kitchen.

'Yes, Jade,' I said. 'Soon.'

'Good luck, love,' said mum. 'Tell his mum and dad I'm praying for him.'

*

Dad went to the reception desk and asked for directions to Ward Twelve.

'Who are you here to see, please?' said the receptionist.

'Daniel Cox,' I said. 'He's on ward twelve.'

She smiled and stood up. 'Go down that corridor, past the gift shop. Then take a right, through some double doors. Go up two flights of stairs and he's on that stretch.'

'Is it signposted?' said dad, looking confused.

'Yes, it is.'

I saw Dan's dad as soon as we entered the ward. He was at the bottom of the corridor, talking to a nurse.

'Down there,' I said, pointing.

'Can you rub some alcohol gel into your hands, please?' said a passing nurse.

We squirted the gel onto our hands and rubbed it in. It was cold and dried almost instantly. We waited a few minutes before Dan's dad had stopped talking. I looked in rooms and saw patients; mainly elderly people. They were lying in their beds, looking into space or out of the window. Some were asleep with their mouths open. One old lady reminded me of photos of my nan. She had curly, silver hair and chubby cheeks and was wearing a pale blue cardigan. She looked at me without moving her head. Some people had oxygen masks on. Some had tubes coming out of their noses and arms. Some had family and friends around them, talking to them, laughing with them or just sat quietly, holding their hands. Others were just by themselves. I wanted to tell all of them that it was going to be OK.

'Stop staring, Jamie,' said dad. 'It's rude.'

Dan's dad saw us and grinned. He shook both of our hands and patted me on the back.

'Great to see you, Jamie. No Teddy with you?'

'He didn't want to come.'

'I understand,' he said. 'Dan's in there.'

He pointed to a room that said NIL BY MOUTH on the door.

'What does that mean?' I said.

'It's to let the nurses know not to feed him,' he said.

'He can't have any food?'

'He can't swallow, Jamie. His throat's too damaged. He's heavily medicated now.' He stopped and dabbed his eyes with his handkerchief. 'He's in no pain, thank God.'

'Can I go in?'

'Of course. Of course. His mum's in there with Milly, our good friend from church.'

'You go in,' said dad. 'I'll wait out here. I'll go and get a coffee or something.'

I opened the door and crept in.

Dan's mum was beside him, stroking his hand. Milly was sat in a chair in the corner, reading a magazine. Photos of family and friends were up on the wall. The card that Mrs Alard got everyone to sign was there, along with a card from all of the teachers. Playing in the background was the relaxing music that Dan had been listening to at home.

Milly looked up from her magazine and smiled at me. She looked over at Dan's mum, who was just gazing at Dan.

'Veronica,' she whispered.

Dan's mum looked up suddenly. She walked over and gave me a hug.

'It's so good to see you, love,' she said, quietly. 'Thank you so much for coming.'

'It's OK,' I said. 'I wanted to see him. How is he?'

'He's just had a little setback with this infection. Once he's shaken it off, he'll be on the road to recovery.'

Dan's eyes were wide open. He lay on top of the sheets, mini pools of sweat on his forehead. An oxygen mask covered his nose and mouth. He was wired up to machines that clicked and beeped. His hands were by his sides. His breathing was the heaviest I'd heard it yet. I suddenly became aware of my own breath and realised I didn't have to think about doing it.

'Does he know I'm here?' I said.

'I should think so.'

She looked into his unblinking eyes.

'Jamie's here, love,' she said. 'He's come to see you. Remember Jamie?'

He looked up.

'That means yes,' she said, proudly.

She removed his oxygen mask. His head turned slightly towards me. He forced half a smile.

I sat down next to him and held his hand. It was lifeless, like an empty glove. I started to talk to him in my head.

'You're going to be OK,' I said. *'It'll soon be over. Your angels will be waiting for you.'*

He coughed violently. His mum shot up and started to rub his back. She put his oxygen mask back over his mouth and nose and he calmed down.

'Come and visit me when you get there,' I said. *'But don't scare me!'*

We stayed in silence for fifteen minutes, listening to the music, accompanied by the added clicks and beeps from the machines. A nurse came in to check on him. She put drops in his eyes and rubbed his eye lids. She saw me watching.

'Stops his eyes from drying up,' she said, smiling at me.

She checked the level of something at the side of his bed and made a note of it.

'If you want anything, Mrs Cox,' she whispered, 'just let me know.'

'Thank you, my dear.'

I asked his mum why his eyes needed drops. She said he couldn't blink. She said by blinking you keep your eyes clean and moist and free from dust, but because he's lost the ability to do that, his eyes were at risk of getting dry and sore.

His dad walked in and said my dad was asking for me.

I nodded.

'I have to go now, Dan,' I said. 'I'll see you soon, OK?'

He looked up.

41

We were silent on the way home. We pulled into the drive and he turned the engine off.

'I'm proud of you, you know,' he said.

I didn't say anything.

'You don't know this... hell, your mum doesn't even know this. But when I was your age, I lost a good friend.'

I looked at him, surprised.

'Robert, his name was,' he said.

He started playing with his keys.

'He was crushed.'

'By what?' I said.

'A forklift truck. We were riding on the side and the driver lost control. It toppled over and crushed him. He died instantly.'

I stared at him, waiting for him to continue.

'It should've been me,' he said. 'It was my idea to go on the damn thing. I knew the driver really well. He was my neighbour. Mr Kenneth, his name was. A good man. He used to let us ride on the side loads of times. It was a laugh. A bit of fun.' He looked at me. 'Boys will be boys, eh.'

I nodded.

'I've never forgiven myself for that.'

We sat in silence for a bit.

'I can remember seeing how upset his parents were. How they looked at me as if I was a murderer. I can still see their eyes now.'

He looked out of his window and wiped his eyes.

'It was an accident,' I said. 'It was just his time to go.'

He nodded. 'I suppose you could look at it like that. I still think about him. I think about what he would look like now, if he was still alive. Would he have had a family of his own? Where would he be working?'

'He's OK where he is,' I said.

Dad looked at me and frowned.

'No,' he said. 'Once you're dead, you're dead. There's none of that life after death crap. It's just wishful thinking, Jamie. That's all it is.'

We got out of the car and he told me to keep quiet about everything he had said.

'Just between us two, yeah?'

He's Casey, I thought to myself. Dad's Casey the caterpillar.

42

I was supposed to go and see Dan again the following Sunday but it never happened. His dad rang the morning before and told me he had passed away. I held the phone away from my ear, motionless.

He was gone.

'Jamie? Are you there?'

I put the phone back to my ear.

'Yes. Yes, I'm here.'

'Are you OK?'

I hesitated.

'Yeah, I'm fine. How are you?'

'We're in shock. We're emotionally and physically drained... completely exhausted. Jamie?'

'Yeah?'

'Please don't become a stranger to us. You're always welcome at ours.'

'Thank you.'

'I'll keep you informed about the funeral.'

*

I went and slouched on the sofa. Jade was eating a slice of toast. She had a plastic cup of milky tea next to her on a buffet.

'Dan's better now, isn't he?'

I wanted to cry but I couldn't.

'Yes, Jade,' I said. 'Finally.'

She jumped up and clapped her hands with excitement.

'What did Dan's dad want at this time in the morning?' said mum, standing in the doorway.

I told her the news and she started to cry. Jade went and hugged her and told her not to worry.

'I'm so sorry, Jamie, love,' said mum. She got a tissue from her sleeve and blew her nose.

'It's OK,' I said. 'I kind of feel relieved for him.'

She looked at me and turned the TV down.

'What do you mean, love?'

'He's not in any pain anymore. He's gone to that place where all there is, is love and light.'

She smiled and walked over and kissed me on the top of my head.

'I have two little angels, don't I.'

'Yes you have,' said Jade.

*

Two hours later, I knocked on Teddy's door. Nobody came. I knocked again and his head appeared at the landing window.

'It's a bit early, man,' he said. His hair was stuck up on one side.

'Come down,' I said.

'Two mins.'

I could hear him thudding down the stairs. He opened the door and invited me in.

'What do you want? What's up?'

I paused. 'Dan died this morning.'

He cried and cried. His mum and dad came into the kitchen and asked what was up. He told them in between sobs. His mum hugged him, making 'shh' noises all the while.

Teddy's dad gave a deep sigh.

'Teddy, try and be happy for Dan,' I said. 'He's in no more pain now.'

His mum said I was right. She said we needed to think of him as being like a bird, being set free from its cage.

Teddy calmed down and blew his nose.

'You going to be OK?' I said.

'Yeah. Thanks for letting me know.'

'I'll let you know about the funeral.'

He nodded and wiped his eyes.

'No age, is that,' said his dad, shaking his head and putting the kettle on. 'No age at all.'

*

On the way home, I went to knock on Mr Legna's door. I wanted to tell him about Dan. There was a note stuck to the back door, flapping about in the wind.

> DEAR JAMIE
> I HEARD ABOUT YOUR FRIEND, DAN
> I TRULY HOPE YOU UNDERSTAND
> I'M OUT VISITING A FRIEND
> I'LL SEE YOU LATER
> MR L

43

That evening, I went round to Dan's. The blinds were still closed but I could see lights on. His mum came to the door. She smiled and held her arms open. She held me close and thanked me for being such a good friend.

'How are you?' I said.

'Tired. Very tired. We both are. It's been a long, long ride. Daniel's safe now, though. He's with God.'

I smiled.

I followed her into the living room.

'It's so quiet, you know,' she said. 'I know he's only been gone a few hours but-'

She started to cry.

I waited a while before speaking.

'Are you OK?' I whispered.

'Yes, I'm fine, love. Do you want a drink and a biscuit?'

'OK. Thank you.'

I joined her in the kitchen.

'I feel more relieved than anything else,' I said.

'So do I, Jamie.' She was on her tiptoes, trying to get the biscuit tin from on top of the fridge.

'I know he's not in any pain now,' I said.

She nodded and filled the kettle.

'You couldn't be more right.'

We sat for half an hour, reminiscing. She showed me photos I had never seen before and told me tales of what he was like as a baby.

'You know, the nurses who came to the house were always amazed at how relaxed he was. You know what I told them?'

I dunked my biscuit in my tea.

'I always said: I'm too blessed to be stressed! They used to laugh at me. That's how I felt, though. I feel so grateful to have been given the opportunity to spend thirteen years with such a happy, wise and loving soul. A true gift, he was.'

44

The following morning, Dan's mum rang me. I was surprised to hear her so happy. She sounded like her old self, before everything happened. Her words came tumbling out.

'He came to me, Jamie! He came to me!'
'What? Dan? Dan did?'
'Yes!'
'What do you mean?'
'I was trying to get to sleep last night and I must've nodded off, because I heard his voice and it woke me. It startled me and I shot up in bed, looking around the room for him. It was as if he was right next to me, right next to my bed.'

We both laughed.

'Wait until you hear this,' she said. 'He said to me, "Mum, the best is yet to come!" He said it with such enthusiasm, too. I *know* it was him. I wanted to hold him but he wasn't there. Now I know he's all right, for sure.'

*

'What were you laughing about?' said mum. 'Wasn't it Dan's mum on the phone?' She looked confused.

I told her what Dan's mum had heard and how certain she was that it was him. Dad walked in when I was halfway through telling her. He stood in the doorway, listening to the end.

'She was dreaming, Jamie,' he said. 'She's in shock. The mind can do crazy things when you're grieving.'

Mum told him to stop being so heartless.

'I'm not being *heart*less,' he snapped. 'I'm being rea*listic*.'

'Well, maybe life and death aren't what you think they are,' I said.

'When you're dead, Jamie, you're dead.'

Jade laughed.

We all stopped and looked at her.

'Silly Daddy,' she said.

45

Mum really wanted me to go shopping with them. Even dad was going. She said they weren't going for anything specific but thought it would be nice if we all went.

'Plus,' she said, 'it'll be good for you to get out and about.'

The only reason I didn't want to go was because I hated shopping. But she assured me we wouldn't be clothes shopping, or even worse, shoe shopping.

'We'll just be looking around, love, that's all. Come on, we'll have fish and chips for lunch. What d'you think?'

Then, without saying a word, Jade took hold of my hand and walked me to the car. She opened the back door and climbed in, onto her booster seat. Mum laughed.

'All set?' said dad, making sure Jade and I had our seatbelts on. Jade gave him a thumbs up.

We reversed out of the driveway and drove past Mr Legna's. Both Jade and I looked for him.

'There he is,' said Jade.

But I didn't see him.

*

That night, I lay staring at the ceiling. Mum and dad had been in bed for about an hour. Thoughts of Dan filled the silence. Where had he gone? I felt the photo of grandad under my pillow and just held it.

'Grandad,' I whispered, 'are you with Dan?'
No answer.

I started to cry but I didn't know why. I squeezed my eyes shut. Almost instantly I started dreaming. I was in a field. It reminded me of Quarry Hill, but much greener, brighter and flatter. I looked up at the sky and could see only blue. There was singing, like a soothing choir. It got carried in the air. It was everywhere and sounded so familiar to me.

'Jamie,' said a voice. It seemed to fill the space all around me.

I turned around. It was Dan. He was standing there, smiling, glowing. He looked like he used to, before he got ill, but even healthier than that.

'This isn't a dream, Jamie,' he said. His lips didn't move. 'This is more real than what you think is real.'

A light started to appear beside him, like an orb. It started to form an outline of a person, but I couldn't see who.

'Please tell my mum she wasn't dreaming,' said Dan. 'Visit her and my dad when you can. They know in their hearts that I'm OK but sometimes they'll need reminding.'

I nodded.

'I have to go,' he said. 'They're calling me.'

'Who are?'

The person next to him was getting filled in with more and more detail, but I still couldn't work out who it was.

'This is just the beginning, Jamie,' he said. 'Death isn't what everybody thinks it is. And when your time comes, don't be afraid. Remember that. You could say you're dying already. You could say that about every single person. And it's perfectly natural and it's perfectly safe.'

I began to laugh and cry at the same time.

'I'm dying!' I shouted. My voice echoed in the distance, bouncing off the light all around me.

Dan waved goodbye as he faded away, along with the figure of light next to him.

'Don't go!' I said.

'Jamie,' he said, 'there's nowhere *to go*.'

*

I woke up smiling. It was morning. I could remember every word Dan had said.

'It wasn't a dream,' I whispered. 'I'm going to die and it's perfectly safe.'

I couldn't stop myself from laughing. I laughed until my eyes watered.

I went downstairs and found Jade sitting in front of the TV, eating toast. Mum came in, holding a bowl of cereal.

'Morning, love,' she said. 'You look like you've had a good night sleep.'

'He spoke to Dan,' said Jade, not taking her eyes off the TV.

I smiled at her but mum frowned.

'He came to me in my sleep, Mum,' I said. 'He told me to keep on visiting his mum and dad. He told me to tell his mum that she wasn't dreaming.'

Mum didn't look convinced.

'He said something else, too: he said we're all dying and it's perfectly safe.'

'Not in front of Jade, love,' said mum.

'But it's true, though, isn't it?' I said. 'We're all dying and we're all going to die.'

'Jamie,' she said, in a tone that I knew to stop talking.

*

After lunch, Jade asked me to play a new game that Dad had played with her.

'Do words backwards,' she said.

She handed me a pen and a piece of paper.

'What do you mean?' I said.

She turned the page over to reveal the words that Dad had already written backwards.

'Bob,' she pointed.

'What's Bob backwards?' I said.

'Bob!' she laughed.

'Dog,' she pointed.

'What's dog backwards?'

'God!' she laughed.

I wrote down Tree and next to it what it was backwards.

'Eert,' I said.

'Eert! she laughed. 'Another one!'

'Bat,' I said, and wrote down tab.

'Tab!' she giggled. 'Another one!'

'You think of one,' I said.

She thought for a while.

'Bun!'

'Nub,' I said, and wrote it down.

She laughed and laughed.
She looked up and held her chin, thinking.
'Angel!' she shouted.
I wrote it down.
'L - E - G - N - A.'
I paused.
'Legna,' I whispered.
I dropped the pen and ran out of the house.
I banged on Mr Legna's door. No answer. I looked through the letter box and shouted for him. There was a heap of post behind the door. I looked through the living room window. Nobody. Nothing. I ran round the back and stood on my tiptoes, peering through the kitchen window. The stove looked as if it hadn't been used for months. The small, white wooden stool was gone and the cupboard doors were hanging off their hinges, revealing brown, mouldy shelves.

I went to the front of the house and looked at the empty shell.

THE END

In memory of my friend, Daniel Cox, who, a week before Christmas, was diagnosed with a brain tumour; who, before he lost his speech, said he saw angels at his bedside, and who, a week after his passing, was heard shouting, 'Mum! The best is yet to come!'

I wish you well, my friend.

ALSO AVAILABLE

The Girl with the Green-Tinted Hair: A Miraculous Fable - Book 1

Happiness & Honey: A Miraculous Fable - Book 2

A Stolen Youth

My Grandad's Hiding Place

Please sign up to my readers' group by visiting my Facebook page and clicking "Sign Up". You'll receive a free copy of the story **The Sun and the Moon**:
facebook.com/gavinwhyteauthor
You can find me on Twitter at:
@Gavinwhyte888

Email: gavinswhyte@gmail.com

Printed in Great Britain
by Amazon